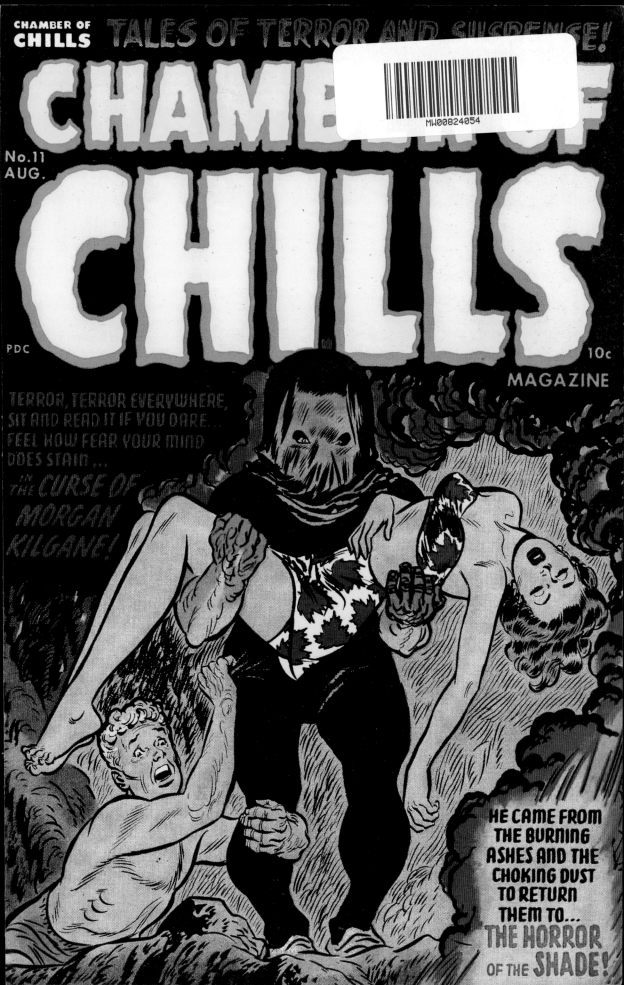

CHAMBER OF CHILLS

IN THIS ISSUE:

NO. 11
AUG.

RETURN FROM BEDLAM

THE GIRL OF THE MOONPOOL

THE CURSE OF MORGAN KILGANE

THE HORROR SHADE!

THE GIRL OF THE MOONPOOL

JON--JON C-A-R-W-A-Y... I BID YOU COME! JON!!

WHAT ARE YOU DOING, JON? ARE YOU CRAZY? THERE'S NO ONE IN THERE!

LET ME GO! I--I'VE GOT TO GO DOWN THERE! CAN'T YOU SEE HER? SHE'S CALLING TO ME!

JON CARWAY HAD BEEN SCOUTING THE COUNTRYSIDE TO PAINT A GOOD LANDSCAPE, WHEN IT HAPPENED...

WELL, I'LL BE--! THERE'S A BEAUTIFUL GIRL IN THAT POOL!

WON'T YOU TAKE A COOL SWIM IN THESE WATERS? PLEASE HEED ME--PLEASE!

I--I MUST BE DREAMING! IT CAN'T BE REAL! SHE'S BEAUTIFUL--BUT IT JUST CAN'T BE REAL!

THERE--! I KNEW IT! IT'S ONLY THE LEAVES FALLING INTO THE WATER THAT MADE ME SEE THE ILLUSION...BUT IT WAS SO BEAUTIFUL--SO BEAUTIFUL!

JON CARWAY WENT HOME AND TRIED TO FORGET IT. BUT THAT NIGHT AT A PARTY GIVEN BY ONE OF HIS FRIENDS, HE HAD TO TELL HIS HOSTS WHAT HAD OCCURRED...

THE IMAGE OF THAT GIRL'S FACE WAS AS CLEAR TO ME AS MINE IS TO YOU!

OH, COME NOW, JON. ADMIT THAT YOU'RE SPOOFING!

BUT BEFORE CARWAY COULD REPLY, A DISTRACTING DUET OF VOICES BROKE INTO THE GENERAL GAIETY OF THE GUESTS. THE BUTLER HAD AN UNWELCOME VISITOR...

LET ME IN-- LET ME IN-- OR YOU'LL BE CURSED!

OUT YOU GO--! GET OUT!

WHAT IS IT, HAWKINS?

IT'S THIS OLD HAG, SIR! SHE WANTS TO COME IN!

AY! WOULD YE CHEAT ME OUT OF MY HAPPINESS? I ONLY WANTED TO BE IN THE MIDST OF ALL THIS YOUTH AND GAIETY. I'M A LONELY OLD WOMAN WHO'S BEEN LIVING ALONE NEAR THE RIVER'S EDGE HERE!

LET HER IN! SHE LOOKS POSITIVELY FAMISHED, POOR THING!

THANK YOU, SIR! MAY FORTUNE SMILE DOWN UPON YOU! BUT I WANT NO FOOD OR SHELTER NOW! INSTEAD--I SHALL GIVE YOU THE SECRET OF THE GIRL IN THE MOONPOOL FOR YOUR KINDNESS!

THE GIRL IN THE-- THE MOONPOOL?

YES! HEH, HEH...LONG, LONG AGO-- SHE AND HER SWEETHEART WERE FLEEING HER FIRST LOVER WHO PURSUED THEM TO THE POOL AND KILLED HIS RIVAL IN A SWORD-FIGHT.

THE GIRL THREW HERSELF IN THE POOL RATHER THAN LIVE. HER BODY WAS NEVER RECOVERED, AND HER FIRST SWEETHEART DIED AFTERWARDS, SHUNNED BY ALL. SINCE THEN, ONLY HANDSOME STRANGERS SEE HER--AND THOSE WHO DO HER BIDDING NEVER RETURN--BUT TO YOU I'LL GIVE THE SECRET!

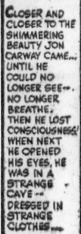

CLOSER AND CLOSER TO THE SHIMMERING BEAUTY JON CARWAY CAME... UNTIL HE COULD NO LONGER SEE-- NO LONGER BREATHE. THEN HE LOST CONSCIOUSNESS! WHEN NEXT HE OPENED HIS EYES, HE WAS IN A STRANGE CAVE -- DRESSED IN STRANGE CLOTHES...

OH, JON--JON, MY SWEETHEART! YOU CAME! YOU HEARD MY CALL!

WHA--? WHERE AM I?

BUT BEFORE HE COULD FIND AN ANSWER TO HIS QUESTIONS, A MUFFLED FIGURE IN BLACK STEPPED FORTH FROM THE SHADOWS!

INTRUDER! YOU HAVE TRESPASSED HERE--AND ONE OF US MUST DIE!

KILL HIM FOR ME, JON! TAKE ME AWAY FROM THIS PRISON!

YES, MY DEAREST!

WHY AM I ANGRY? STRANGE WORDS ARE POURING FORTH FROM MY LIPS! HIS FACE--IT LOOKS LIKE ONE OF THE FACES I SAW BEFORE! I CAN'T CONTROL MYSELF! I MUST KILL HIM!

DIE!

AIIIEEEE!

HA, HA, HA... IT IS DONE THE CURSE IS RENEWED ONCE MORE!

NO SOONER HAD HIS SWORD RUN THROUGH THE MAN'S CHEST, THAN THE FIGURE DISSOLVED INTO NOTHINGNESS--SCREAMING AND SHRIEKING WITH A TERROR BEYOND DESCRIPTION.

T-THE MAN IS DIS-APPEARING--AND--AND THE GIRL IS DIVING BACK INTO THE WATER AGAIN! NO--WAIT!

I'VE GOT TO STOP HER! I'VE GOT TO MAKE SENSE OUT OF THIS!

NO! YOU KNOW NOT WHAT YOU DO! DO NOT WANT HER!

SHE IS EVIL!

STOP! AIIIEEE! HE IS ALMOST UPON HER!

I SEEM TO HEAR VOICES IN MY HEAD! IT--IT MUST BE MY IMAGINATION! I'M NEARLY UP TO HER! ALMOST--ALMOST!

4

MEANWHILE, JON CARWAY'S FRIEND LET OUT A SIGH OF RELIEF AS HE WATCHED A HEAD BREAK THE SURFACE OF THE WATER...

JON! THANK GOD YOU'RE ALIVE! BUT YOU'VE BEEN UNDER FOR MORE THAN *TEN* MINUTES!

I FOUND HER, MIKE! I FOUND HER!

I--GOOD LORD! THIS IS SEA-WEED! WHERE DID SHE GO?

JON--ARE--ARE YOU SURE YOU'RE ALL RIGHT?

COME ON--LET'S GET OUT OF HERE--FAR--FAR AWAY!

SOMEHOW, JON CARWAY MANAGED TO GET HOME--SOMEHOW, HE MANAGED TO MAKE A SUPERFICIALLY-LOGICAL EXPLANATION OF WHAT HAD OCCURRED, BUT IN HIS OWN MIND, HE KNEW THE TRUTH--HE KNEW SOMETHING OCCULT HAD HAPPENED THAT NEXT MORNING...

I CAN'T GET *HER* OUT OF MY MIND! IT WAS REAL--AS REAL AS THE SUN! YET--DID I DREAM THIS? I'VE GOT TO GET HOLD OF MYSELF!

HELLO, JON! I DID AS YOU SAID. I TRIED TO FIND OUT WHERE THE OLD HAG LIVED--BUT THERE'S NO SIGN OF HER--AND NO ONE ELSE KNOWS ABOUT HER! HEY--ARE YOU OKAY?

YEAH--I--I GUESS I AM! SOMEHOW, I KNEW YOU WOULDN'T FIND HER AGAIN! I KNEW...

HE DECIDED TO FORGET ABOUT IT. BUT, A FEW HOURS LATER, WHEN HE WAS TRYING TO REST ON THE PORCH...

JON--*JON CARWAY! HEAR ME! I COMMAND YOU TO RETURN!*

AAAGHH! THAT VOICE! IT'S COMING FROM THE POOL!

16

WHERE ARE WE? WHY HAVE YOU BROUGHT US *HERE??*

YOU WILL NOT FIND LIFE AS *COMFORTABLE* IN VARSUVIA AS IN YOUR WORLD! THE HEAT IS *OPPRESSIVE* AND THE DAYS ARE... *NUMBERED!!*

CAUGHT IN THE *RED NIGHTMARE* OF A *CRUMBLING* AND *FORBIDDING* WORLD, THE COUPLE ARE DRAGGED BY THE DEMONIAC VALBORG THROUGH SCENES THAT FREEZE THE BLOOD AND SEAR THE MIND!...

SEE! YOU ARE PRIVILEGED TO BEHOLD THE *DYING THROES* OF A CIVILIZATION BEING BURNED TO ASHES BY FIRES SUCH AS THIS!

THERE MUST BE SOME WAY OUT OF THIS LIVING HELL! WE MUST FIND IT!

NO! YOU CANNOT ESCAPE NOW! I WON'T *LET* YOU RETURN TO YOUR HAPPY LIFE BEYOND THIS ACCURSED KINGDOM!!

LET ME GO! LET ME GO!!

COME, WE SHALL LEAP TOGETHER INTO THE FLAMES!!.... WHY WAIT FOR THE FIRES TO SPREAD LIKE A *PLAGUE* AND *DEVOUR* US UNAWARES??

YAAAH-H-H!!! NO!! DON'T--!!

*S*UDDENLY THE CRACKED VOICE OF THE OLD HAG SOUNDS THROUGH THE MURKY AIR--AS VALBORG STANDS POISED WITH HIS VICTIM ABOVE THE SULPHUR PIT!...

STOP!

WHAT IS YOUR WISH, MID-NIGHT HAG??

YOU KNOW FULL WELL, VALBORG, THAT IF SOMEONE *OTHER* THAN AN INHABITANT OF VARSUVIA ENTERS THE FLAMES OF THE PIT-- THE EARTH WILL *CRUMBLE TO DUST* ABOUT OUR FEET!!

WHY NOT *NOW* RATHER THAN *LATER?* WE ARE A DOOMED RACE! I SHALL DESTROY WHOM I PLEASE!!

4

YOU HAVE ABUSED MY *GIFT*, VALBORG-- AND FOR THAT YOU MUST *DIE*!!

NO! I DIDN'T MEAN IT! I'LL LET THEM RETURN! N--

AIEE-EE!

YOU MUST HELP US RETURN, OLD WOMAN! WE DON'T BELONG IN THIS *ROTTING LAND*!

AH, SIR, YOU ARE *RIGHT!* VARSUVIA IS NOT FOR THE LIVING BUT FOR THE *DAMNED* SUCH AS VALBORG!! THE FLAMES ARE THEIR REWARDS!

MAY YOU *NEVER REMEMBER* THIS NIGHT-- AND THE WRETCHED SOULS OF THIS LOST WORLD! ONLY THEN WILL YOUR HEARTS STAY FREE OF THE SCORCHING HORROR OF VESUVIA!!

FOR THE LAST TIME, THE HEAVENS *QUAKE*--AS IF *ASTONISHED* BY THE FIGURES THAT HURTLE THROUGH THEIR ETERNAL STILLNESS!!

AND IN A MATTER OF SECONDS, THE YOUNG COUPLE ARE AMID *NORMAL* SURROUNDINGS...

JEAN, IS--IS IT POSSIBLE THAT VARSUVIA WAS H...

...OH, DAVID, DOES THIS MEAN THAT EVIL IS BEING DESTROYED AND THAT VALBORG WAS THE...

TO LIVE AGAIN!

"If this process works, Damos, I shall be young again. I shall be able to live again!"

"Yes, Pithian, and the world will gape with admiration at us. We shall be acclaimed the greatest scientists the world has ever known. We shall have given the world the secret of eternal life...the secret of being young forever!"

Damos' hand struck out as a cobra. It curled itself about a lever and pulled back. Instantly, the room was plunged into a chasm of exploding sparks and thundering noises. Jagged streams of electricity played about a suspended flask which bubbled a brilliant purple.

The lever was pushed to its original position.

"I will lay down on the table, Pithian. Adjust the head plate and then begin injecting the solution into my arm. According to our calculations, when you take the plate away, I will be a different man...a young man!"

The head plate was adjusted.

The transfusion apparatus was installed and, as the second hand of the laboratory clock passed the *two*, the bottle containing the revolutionary solution began to drain of its contents.

The second hand passed the *three*...the *four* ...the *six*...the *nine!*

"It is all over. I m-must r-remove the head plate!"

Pithian's trembling hands slowly lifted the concealing iron plate.

"Ahhhhh..."

"Hello, Pithian! I can see by your face that the experiment has succeeded. Here, help me, hurry!"

The man that stood before Pithian was a young man, shot through with the strength of youth. That he had been a sixty-year-old man but minutes before was nowhere in evidence!

"Remarkable!"

"Unbelievable, you mean, Pithian! But, we are not yet finished. There is one more thing to be done!"

"What is that, Damos?"

"This!"

"Ugghhhh!"

Damos had driven a dagger deep into the chest of Pithian.

"You fool! Do you think I would let you share in the wealth to be soon gotten from our solution! I am young now and life holds no limits for me!"

With the cool movement of one who has planned for months, Damos went about completing his plan. Then, an hour later...

"I am finished. All I...haaaaaa, ha, ha!"

"Yaaaaaaaaaaaaaaaa!"

"Crazy! Crazy! Crazy!"

"Men in white! Men in white! Men in white!"

Damos had gone insane!

His deranged mind could never know why! But the answer was simple.

In every so-called perfect crime, there must exist one flaw. That is so because a human being can never be perfect and so must commit an error, however small. Damos had committed an error.

"Crazy! Crazy! Crazy! Haaaaaaaaaaa!"

Damos had forgotten that during his earlier days, he had gone insane because of overwork. Only expert care and a long rest were able to restore his mind to its original state. Damos had forgotten that the rejuvenating solution would propel him back in time to just about the age when he had gone insane.

In other words, Damos was experiencing the same condition now that he did then!

As he reeled from wall to wall, he had little chance to see what was happening.

"Haaaaaa! Men in white!"

Damos' hands were becoming gnarled with age. His mind was already split with insanity but now it was evident that the solution did not work...permanently!

STRANGE LEGENDS

ETCHED IN TIME, THE LEGENDS OF THE WORLD HAVE LONG AMAZED THOSE WHO HAVE HEARD OF THEM. SUCH IS THE LEGEND OF "THE GREAT DROUGHT AND THE WATERS OF WACO!"

IT WAS THE TIME OF THE TERRIBLE DROUGHT IN THE SOUTHWESTERN UNITED STATES. A COLONY OF SPANIARDS WHO HAD BEEN MINING PRECIOUS METALS COULD NOT STAND THE BLAZING SUN AND THE DRY RIVER BEDS ANYMORE. THEY BEGAN TO MOVE...

AS THE DAYS PASSED AND THE HEAT OF THE SUN'S RAYS ATE INTO MAN AND ANIMAL ALIKE, THE SPANIARDS KNEW THAT THEIR HEAVY BAGS OF BULLION WOULD HAVE TO BE LEFT BEHIND! SO TWO SMALL CAVES WERE DUG IN THE SIDE OF THE HILL AND THE BULLION LEFT THERE...

FINALLY, THE SPANIARDS' TRAIL, DOTTED WITH DEATH, LED THEM TO THE LAND OF THE WACO INDIANS, WHERE THEY SAW A GREAT RIVER FLOWING, FRESH AND CLEAR...

THE EMIGRANTS GAVE THE RIVER THE NAME OF LOS BRAZOS DE DIOS---THE ARMS OF GOD. AND, THERE, THEY BUILT A SETTLEMENT WHERE THEY COULD WAIT UNTIL THE DROUGHT ENDED, SO THAT THEY COULD RETURN HOME...

BUT, TROUBLE SEEMED TO STALK THE SPANIARDS. ONE DAY, A MARAUDING GROUP OF INDIANS FROM THE NORTH CREPT DOWN ON THE COLONY. BEFORE THE FRIENDLY WACOS COULD HELP, THE RENEGADES HAD WIPED OUT THE WHITES TO THE CHILD!

ONLY ONE MAN CAME OUT ALIVE FROM THE SLAUGHTER AND HE DIED SOON AFTER. WHAT HAPPENED TO THE BULLION THAT WAS BURIED IN THE HILL? WHAT HAPPENED TO THE SPANIARDS' FABULOUSLY RICH MINES? NO ONE KNOWS! THE DESERT SANDS HAVE CLAIMED WHAT IS THEIRS!

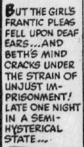

BUT THE GIRL'S FRANTIC PLEAS FELL UPON DEAF EARS...AND BETH'S MIND CRACKS UNDER THE STRAIN OF UNJUST IMPRISONMENT! LATE ONE NIGHT IN A SEMI-HYSTERICAL STATE...

MY LONG DEAD GREAT GRANDMOTHER! IF YOU HEAR ME LET ME SEE YOU NOW! FOR I MUST ESCAPE FROM BEDLAM!

SWOOSH!

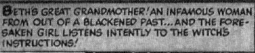

BETH'S GREAT GRANDMOTHER! AN INFAMOUS WOMAN FROM OUT OF A BLACKENED PAST...AND THE FORESAKEN GIRL LISTENS INTENTLY TO THE WITCH'S INSTRUCTIONS!

NOW DRINK THIS, MY CHILD! THE RESULTS SHOULD BE EXTRAORDINARY...AND SATISFYING! HEE-HEE!

HEE-HEE-HEE! EXCELLENT, MY CHILD! EXCELLENT! NOW AWAIT THE RESULTS!

IT...IT... OOOOOHHHH! WHAT....

SWOOSH

GROAN!

THE NEXT MORNING...

THIS IS ABOUT THE ONLY WAY THEY LEAVE BEDLAM ...IN A BOX!

YES...NO ONE EVER ... EEEK! I SAW... IT... MOVE!

MADDENED, GAUNT AND BENT UPON REVENGE, THE GIRL MAKES HER WAY BACK TO THE INN WHERE SHE SECRETS HERSELF IN AN UNDERGROUND CHAMBER...

HEE-HEE! REVENGE UPON THE WEEKS BROTHERS! GREAT GRANDMOTHER, INSTRUCT ME IN ITS EXECUTION!

SWOOSH!

YOU ASK FOR REVENGE, SO YOU SHALL HAVE IT! *HEE-HEE!!* THESE MISERABLE VISIONS OF YOUR CONTAINMENT! I RELEASE THEM IN YOUR CUSTODY, MY DEAR!

SPLENDID! WE'LL SEE HOW THE WEEKS BROTHERS WELCOME THEM!

WHAT THE--- *AIIEEEEE!*

HEE-HEE! IT'S ME, KEITH! YOUR SISTER-IN-LAW, BETH! REMEMBER ME?!

HORRIFIED BY THE GHOULISH SPECTACLE, THE VILLAINOUS KEITH BOLTS WILDLY FROM HIS HOME WITH BETH AND THE HIDEOUS VISIONS IN CLOSE PURSUIT!

NO! YOU'LL NEVER GET ME! *NO!*

A DESERVED DEATH! *HEE-HEE!* BUT COME! THERE ARE OTHERS!

AIIEEEEEE

OTHERS? OF COURSE! SURELY YOU REMEMBER EPHRAM! IF YOU DON'T, BETH *DOES!*

NO! I'M IMAGINING IT! MORE HORRIBLE THAN BEDLAM ITSELF! IT CAN'T...!

BUT IT IS, EPHRAM!

NO! I'M GOING MAD! MAD! I CAN'T STAND IT ANY LONGER! THERE'S NO PLACE TO HIDE! THEY'RE EVERYWHERE!

EPHRAM'S MIND SNAPS AS DID BETH'S BEFORE HIM...AND A STRANGE, SORDID JUSTICE IS HIS REWARD FOR HIS PARTICIPATION IN THE FIENDISH PLOT THAT SENT BETH PATRICK TO BEDLAM!

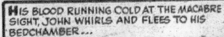

IN THE INN ITSELF, JOHN WEEKS CRINGES IN ABJECT TERROR! CONVINCED THAT HE TOO WILL BE NEXT ON BETH'S LIST, HER HUSBAND PREPARES TO ESCAPE THE DESTINY THAT DESTROYED HIS BROTHERS.

I HAVE THE MONEY! I'LL LEAVE NOW! HA-HA!

NO! NO! AIEE-EE!

YES, JOHN, YES! IT IS ME--BETH! HAVE YOU FORGOTTEN? HEE-HEE!

HIS BLOOD RUNNING COLD AT THE MACABRE SIGHT, JOHN WHIRLS AND FLEES TO HIS BEDCHAMBER...

YOU'LL NEVER GET ME!

HA-HA! BOLTED AND SHUT!

BUT THE WEIRD CREATURES ARE EVERYWHERE AND HYSTERICAL WITH FEAR, JOHN WEEKS CONTINUES HIS HEADLONG FLIGHT!

HEE-HEE! WE'RE COMING, JOHN! BEDLAM WAS LIKE THIS! HEE-HEE!

AR-ROOOO

NO! NO! KEEP AWAY! BETH! IF IT IS YOU--- PLEASE! I ....

IT'S ME, JOHN! HAVE YOU FORGOTTEN YOUR WIFE?

BUT DESPERATION TRANSCENDS HIS FEAR AND THE VENEMOUS WEEKS FEVERISHLY STRUGGLES TO THWART THE GRUESOME BAND THAT FACES HIM!

COALS! AND RED HOT LOGS FOR YOU! SEE HOW YOU LIKE THESE! HA-HA!

TRY THESE!! YOU'RE DEALING WITH JOHN WEEKS NOW!

ARG-H-H-HHH

THIS ISN'T ONE OF MY BROTHERS! IT'S JOHN WEEKS WHO...AGGRAA!

BUT THE FLAMES THAT SAVE WEEKS FROM THE NIGHTMARE THAT HAD STALKED HIM ARE ALSO RESPONSIBLE FOR HIS OWN JUST DEATH...AND BETH PATRICK, HER REVENGE COMPLETE, RISES TO JOIN HER GREAT GRANDMOTHER...! The End

THE CURSE OF MORGAN KILGANE

A HALF FORGOTTEN KNIFE AND A CURIOUS SCROLL... TRANSFORMED BY A MADMAN INTO A COMBINATION FOR VIOLENT DEATH!

JEREMIAH ZARNEAU WAS A WITHDRAWN, EMBITTERED MAN WHO OPERATED A DILAPIDATED ANTIQUE AND CURIOSITY SHOP. MANY STRANGE ITEMS PASSED THROUGH HIS HANDS, BUT NONE MORE SO THAN A WORN, HANDWRITTEN DOCUMENT WRAPPED ABOUT AN ORNATE, HAND-CARVED KNIFE...

STRANGE LOOKING, INDEED....AND TO THINK I FOUND THEM IN AN OLD BUREAU DRAWER.

JEREMIAH ZARNEAU ANTIQUES~

ANTIQUES

BRIC-A-BRAC

VOTE

FASCINATING! PERHAPS OF LITTLE VALUE, BUT FASCINATING!

THEN, THE OLD MAN'S SLIT-LIKE EYES PEER INTENTLY AT THE HAND-WRITTEN DOCUMENT... YELLOWED WITH TIME... AND WRITTEN BY THE LATE FINANCIER MORGAN KILGANE HIMSELF!

IT SAYS THAT HIS FABULOUS WEALTH BE DIVIDED EQUALLY AMONG HIS REMAINING HEIRS, THOUGHT TO BE THREE IN NUMBER!

IT ALSO SAYS OLD KILGANE MADE THIS STRANGE BLADE HIMSELF! AND THAT IT POSSESSES A MYSTIC POWER ENABLING IT TO KILL ANY AND ALL SURVIVING MEMBERS OF THE KILGANE CLAN! INTERESTING INDEED! HEH-HEH!

ZARNEAU'S BREATH COMES IN SHORT GASPS AND HIS PULSE QUICKENS AS HE READS ON, AND HIS NIMBLE, DIABOLICAL MIND CONCEIVES A FIENDISH SCHEME!

..."AND THAT WHOEVER POSSESSES IT CAN DICTATE TO THE KNIFE AND CONTROL THE DESTINIES OF THE KILGANE CLAN!"

SO! WITH THIS SUPERB BLADE I, JEREMIAH ZARNEAU, CAN SOON BECOME MASTER OF ALL MORGAN KILGANE'S MAGNIFICENT WEALTH! IT SHALL BEFIT ME! HA-HA!

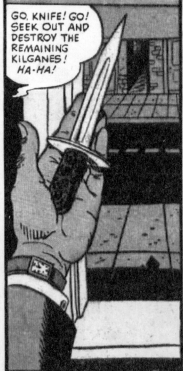

STEEPED IN GREED AND LUST, THE ANTIQUE DEALER PLACES HIS DIABOLICALLY CONCEIVED PLAN INTO DEADLY ACTION!

GO, KNIFE! GO! SEEK OUT AND DESTROY THE REMAINING KILGANES! HA-HA!

AND AS STATED IN THE ANCIENT SCROLL, THE GLISTENING BLADE OBEYS!

2

...AND THE REMAINING HEIRS TO KILGANE'S FORTUNE ARE SLAUGHTERED SILENTLY... AND SAVAGELY...!

IN A NEARBY SUBURB...

LATER THAT NIGHT...

EEEYII!!

THUD!

ITS FIENDISH MISSION COMPLETE, THE AWESOME BLADE RETURNS TO ITS MASTER AND DROPS QUIETLY AT HIS SIDE!

WELL DONE, KNIFE! WELL DONE! NOW TO FORGE THE NECESSARY PAPERS AND PRESENT MYSELF TO THE LEGAL CUSTODIAN OF KILGANE'S ESTATE AS ITS RIGHTFUL HEIR! HA-HA-HA!

AND WITH THIS FORGED SIGNATURE I MAKE THE WEALTH ACCUMULATED OVER HALF A CENTURY MINE!

THESE PAPERS ARE CERTAINLY IN ORDER, SIR! THE KILGANE ESTATE AND FORTUNE ARE RIGHTFULLY YOURS BEYOND A DOUBT!

I THANK YOU, SIR!

AND HERE ARE THE KEYS TO THE MANSION! OF COURSE, YOU KNOW THAT A FOURTH KILGANE HEIR HAS ALWAYS BEEN RUMORED TO EXIST, BUT SINCE HE'S NEVER APPEARED THERE'S NO NEED TO BOTHER ABOUT THAT NOW, IS THERE...

TRIUMPHANTLY, THE MADDENED CURIOSITY DEALER TAKES POSSESSION OF THE RENOWNED MANSION!

HA-HA-HA! THE KILGANE MANSION! YOU'RE MINE NOW! TAKE A GOOD LOOK AT ME! YOUR NEW LORD! JEREMIAH ZARNEAU!

HA-HA-HA-HA! MINE! IT'S ALL MINE! MY WEALTH SHALL BE MY POWER! I SHALL BE MASTER OF MANKIND!

SO! A PORTRAIT IN THE LIVING ROOM...OF KILGANE HIMSELF, NO DOUBT! MEET THE NEW LORD, KILGANE! YOUR WORTHY SUCCESSOR!

BUT AS ZARNEAU PEERS AT THE PORTRAIT, HIS HYSTERICAL TRIUMPH IS QUICKLY TRANS-FORMED INTO ABJECT HORROR AS HE OBSERVES THE UNDENIABLE RESEMBLANCE!

THAT FACE! IT'S...IT'S LIKE MY OWN! NO! *THE FOURTH MISSING RELATIVE!* CAN I...!? NO!

STUNNED AND FROZEN WITH FEAR, ZARNEAU PEERS AT HIS OWN DISTRAUGHT FEATURES IN THE NEARBY MIRROR!

CAN IT REALLY BE? AM *I* THE MISSING HEIR!

BUT THE MIRROR REFLECTS ONLY IMMINENT DEATH!

THE KNIFE! NO! AIIIIEEE!

AND THE *FATEFUL BLADE* THAT HAD DONE THE MADMAN'S BIDDING, IS ITSELF RESPONSIBLE FOR HIS DEATH!

YAGHAAA

THE END

5

GRAVEYARD OF GEMS!

"This is the craziest stunt you've pulled yet!" shuddered Lefty Ciento. "I like dough just as much as you do, Frankie—but robbin' *graves* for it just ain't my style!"

Frankie Gordell threw his partner a disgusted glance. "You're just plain yellow!" he sneered. "Why, that batty old galoot, LeNormand, was buried with close to a million bucks worth of jewels in his coffin! It said so in all the newspapers! He was nuttier than a fruit-cake, I guess ...fixin' his will so that his heirs couldn't collect unless they buried his *gem collection* with him! But his looniness is gonna make *us* millionaires! So, quit snivelin', and let's go!"

So, heads bowed against the cold, screaming wind that sobbed through the dark cemetery, the two hoodlums climbed awkwardly over the low stone wall before them. Now they were amid the graves! The damp, dank tombstones cast eerie shadows on the ground in the pale, icy moonlight. And the sound of sighs—long, low, mournfully-whispering sighs—was everywhere.

"Th—there it is!" croaked Frankie, pointing to a tall, gray monument marked simply, *ABEL LENORMAND*. The sighs grew louder as they approached the freshly-turned mound of earth. Even the wind seemed to wail more shrilly, and the grass rustled beneath their feet as though a thousand unseen insects were slithering through it. Lefty Ciento's hand shook as he raised the shaded lantern he held.

In the flickering, murky lantern light, the inscription on Abel LeNormand's tomb was plain to read. *"Beware, all ye who seek to trespass here,"* it said, *"lest you unleash the fury of a thousand demons of hell, a fury more evil than aught you have yet dreamed!"*

"L—let's get out of here!" gasped Lefty. "It ain't worth it..."

"Grab your shovel, and start diggin'!" grated his partner. "No mess of fancy words is gonna scare *me* off!"

Frankie's own spade made soft, sucking little noises as it dug into the damp black earth. And, after a moment's hesitation, Lefty's shovel joined the chorus. The wind whipped around them, as if screaming in protest against the desecration of the grave, but still they kept on. Sweating and swearing, their backs aching from the strain of their ghoulish labors, the two men dug deeper and deeper. Until at last the final spadeful of dirt was turned, and the long, black coffin lay exposed to the clutching fingers of the moonlight.

"Just got to get that top up now!" panted Lefty, his fears wholly forgotten in the wild, half-hysterical frenzy of his efforts.

Together, the men pulled and tugged at the coffin's lid. And then...

"Aaaaaargh!!" The casket flew open, expos-

ing a king's ransom of jewels and precious gems! Rings, bracelets, crowns, brooches, necklaces of every size, shape and description, along with uncut stones of immense size and dazzling beauty flashed bloody fire in the moonlight! And leaping bolt upright in the midst of all this treasure was the gaunt, ghostly figure of Abel LeNormand!!

But what a figure he was! Towering at least eight feet tall above the cowering thieves, there was no shape, no solidity to his body! Only the faint, wavering outlines of a man, the moonlight gleaming through his flesh, his face a contorted mask of death, his abnormally-long fingers reaching out into the night, clutching at the looters of his grave!

"You were warned!" he screamed. "And you did not heed! So now you will know the tortures of the eternal damned! Now you will know..."

"NO! NO!" screamed his victims. "We'll leave you alone...in peace..."

But it was too late. The ghost of Abel LeNormand called once...twice...and from every piece of jewelry in his coffin, dark, twisted shapes arose. Closer and closer they moved—hundreds of them—closer to the horror-stricken men. They spoke no words, and yet the air around them was filled with sounds, shuddering, screaming sounds such as no human was ever meant to hear! The stench of them grew stronger and stronger, the stench of brimstone and burnt human flesh! Hot, dry fingers clutched at Frankie Gordell and Lefty Ciento, fingers that sunk into their flesh like red-hot razor blades, fingers that pushed and pulled...pushed and pulled...until with one last tug, they dragged the screaming men *into the open grave with them!*

Then, while the shrieks of the doomed souls below still rent the air, the earth slid back into place, and Abel LeNormand's grave looked once more untouched by human hands!

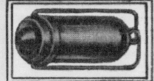

CHAMBER OF CHILLS

CONTENTS
SEPT. NO. 12

THE INNER CIRCLE

You have passed through the Door of Darkness and now you are caught in the CHAMBER OF CHILLS! The demons of the night weave a loathesome pattern in their eerie dance of doom . . . Vultures bite at rotting flesh . . . Witches wail a song of horror . . . Vampires drink in their salvation!

The unknown lies open before you . . . and it is too late to turn back.

But before we go on through the CHAMBER OF CHILLS, let us answer some of your queries.

Many of you have asked about tree-worship and of the spirits that live in the trees.

It is only natural that your European ancestors would pay worship to trees. The trees were everywhere . . . forests covered the length and breadth of the Continent . . . and their arms stretched out to grab all.

At Grbalj in Dalmatia, people say that any who would dare fell a tree must die on the spot! Bleeding and shrieking trees occur often in Chinese literature and are spoken of in many

Oriental history books.

Volumes could be filled with this fascinating and TRUE topic. But the fire is already burning and the phantoms twist in mad frenzy.

We can hold you no longer . . . but continue to send in your questions. Perhaps yours will be answered next month and your letter may be printed.

Yes, it is time now, time to fall into the eddy of evil and whirl into the suspense that waits in the . . .

CHAMBER OF CHILLS!

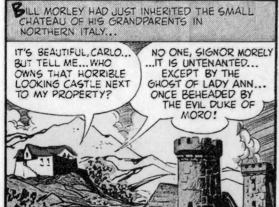

EACH DAY THE DREAM RECURRED...AND EACH TIME HE FOUGHT TO FORGET IT...BUT NOW IT WAS GROWING STEADILY WORSE...

BILL MORELY...LISTEN TO ME...LISTEN...

NO! NO!

NO!

UNABLE TO FIGHT THE SET OF GRUESOME EVENTS THAT CONSTANTLY TORTURED HIS WRETCHED MIND, THE YOUNG AMERICAN QUESTIONED THE FRIGHTENED VILLAGERS ABOUT THE DREAM...

ALL WE KNOW IS THAT THE GIRL WAS THE LAST OWNER OF THE MORO CASTLE! NOW LET US IN PEACE!

THEN MORELY EXAMINED THE RECORDS IN THE ANCIENT LIBRARY...

HERE IT IS. LADY ANN GODWINA POLERA...AND HER FATHER...WERE MURDERED BY ENQIRO STUCCI...THE BLACK DUKE OF MALBA...

THEN THAT GIANT BLACK FIGURE IN MY DREAMS MUST HAVE BEEN...! YES...THAT'S IT! SOMEHOW...THE PAST HAS COME BACK TO TELL ME OF THOSE EVENTS! THE ANSWER *MUST* LIE IN *MORO CASTLE!*

THAT NIGHT, BILL AND AN OLD VILLAGER ENTERED THE EERIE CONFINES OF THE BLACK, FOREBODING CASTLE...

LOOK, PAISAN! HERE...AMONG THE DUST AND COBWEBS...IT'S A SECRET PANEL FILLED WITH TOMES OF WRITING!

AY! 'TIS THE CURSE OF THE DAMNED UPON THEM! SIGNOR...LET US NOT TARRY LONGER!

CAST OFF YOUR HOPES...YOUR DREAMS...YOUR LIFE...FOR THE EVIL MONSTER HAS MURDERED US ALL. I AM THE VERY LAST...A SERVANT IN MY LADY'S GRACES. ALAS... SHE HAS BEEN BEHEADED WITH HER FATHER...AND NOW SHE ROAMS THE GROUNDS FOR VENGEANCE!

SO, THE DREAM WAS REAL IN SUBSTANCE AFTER ALL! IT SAYS FURTHER IN THE BOOK THAT THE EVIL DUKE CAN ONLY BE BEATEN IN PEACETIME!

WHY DO YOU BREAK OFF A SMALL BRANCH OF THAT OLIVE TREE...THE UNIVERSAL SYMBOL OF PEACE? BAH! YOU ARE CRAZY, YOUNG MAN! I LEAVE YOU NOW!

BUT BILL MORELY WAS NOT CRAZY IN THE WAY THE OLD VILLAGER THOUGHT. HE HAD A FANTASTIC PLAN TO AID THE BEAUTIFUL APPARITION ...FOR HE WAS HOPELESSLY IN *LOVE* WITH HER. THAT NEXT NIGHT...

BILL MORELY...! YOU ARE AWAKE! YOU HAVE LEARNED ALL... AND NOW YOU ARE AWAKE! OH... THANK THE MIGHTY ONES!

YES, LADY ANN... I KNOW WHO YOU ARE...BUT WHAT MUST I DO?

FOLLOW ME, MORTAL! IT IS IMPERATIVE THAT YOU ACCOMPLISH WHAT YOU MUST BY DAWN...OTHERWISE, ALL IS LOST...AND I SHALL BE DOOMED TO WANDER IN THIS WORLD FOR ANOTHER SEVEN YEARS!

WE'RE GOING INTO THE SAME COURTYARD I REMEMBER IN MY DREAMS!

BUT SUDDENLY...EVERYTHING BECAME HAZY FOR A MOMENT AND WHEN NEXT HE OPENED HIS EYES...

WHA...?! I'M CLOTHED AS A KNIGHT OF BYGONE DAYS! WHERE'S LADY ANN? AND...WHO ARE THOSE PEOPLE?

BEFORE HE COULD FIND OUT, A COSTUMED, GHOSTLY LACKEY STEPPED FORTH WITH A MAGNIFICENT WHITE STALLION ARMORED AND BEDECKED IN GLITTERING JEWELS AND HANDED HIM THE REIGNS...

MOUNT HIM, SIRRAH! ALL AWAIT DELIVERANCE FROM THE HORROR ASTRIDE THE BLACK CHARGER. IT IS *HE* WHOM YOU MUST FIGHT... *THE BLACK FIGURE!*

WELL I'LL BE...! IT'S THE GIANT WITH THE BLOODY SWORD!

HE'S COMING TOWARDS ME WITH THAT BARBED LANCE OF HIS! HE'S GETTING CLOSER... CLOSER... CLOSER...

SNAP!

ARRGH!

HE'S GOING INSIDE THE CASTLE! I WONDER IF HE COULD BE THE EVIL DUKE OF MALBA?

PAST SLIMY, ROTTING, FUNGUS-COVERED WALLS AND FLICKERING TORCHES THAT CAST DISTORTED, CRAZY SHADOWS, HE SPED...UNTIL HE HAD ENTERED A VAST UNDERGROUND CAVERN....

I'VE NEVER BEEN HERE BEFORE! WHERE IS THAT FIEND LEADING ME TO?

BILL MORELY WAS SOON TO FIND OUT...FOR THE MINUTE HE TOUCHED THE GROUND OF THE CAVERN...

THE FLOOR...IT'S SLIDING OUT FROM UNDER ME!!

R R R R R R R R

HA HA HA...YOU SHALL NOT ESCAPE NOW! YOU HAVE SEALED YOUR OWN DOOM!

I-I CAN'T GET OUT! THE MORE I STRUGGLE THE DEEPER I'M PULLED IN! MY SKIN BURNS... IT MUST BE AN ACID OF SOME SORT!

I-IT'S RISING MORE AND MORE! GOT TO KEEP MY HEAD ABOVE IT... GOT IT...

IT WILL BUBBLE OVER AND TAKE YOU WITH IT. YOU HAVE GAMBLED AND LOST, MORTAL! YOUR SOUL SHALL JOIN THE OTHERS IN THE CASTLE OF THE DAMNED! I LEAVE YOU TO YOUR FATE! HA HA HA!

THE MYSTERIOUS FLUID BUBBLED UP TOWARDS HIS EYES. IN ANOTHER SECOND IT WOULD BE ALL OVER! BUT...

TAKE MY HAND! I CAN SAVE YOU...FOR ONLY THE DOOMED ONES HAVE POWER OVER THE PIT OF *DEATH!*

WHEW! AM I GLAD TO SEE YOU!

BUT WHERE WERE YOU ALL THIS TIME? I'D LIKE A FEW EXPLANATIONS OF THESE WEIRD INCIDENTS!

THERE IS NO TIME NOW ...OHH...LOOK! WE ARE LOST! THE SLAVES OF THE MIGHTY ONE APPROACH!

RUN... FLEA FROM THEM!

THE HEADLESS *KNIGHTS!* BUT WHO ARE THEY? WHAT IS ALL THIS!

MORELY, HOWEVER, DIDN'T WAIT TO FIND OUT! TUGGING AT THE SLENDER FORM BEHIND HIM, HE PULLED HER INTO THE DARKEST RECESSES...

OH! THEY CANNOT BE TRICKED!

THAT PILE OF SKULLS! NOW...I'M BEGINNING TO UNDERSTAND!

SUDDENLY, THE HEADLESS CREATURES WERE UPON THEM! SECONDS LATER, A STRUGGLING MORELY AND THE FRIGHTENED GIRL, WERE LED TOWARDS THE SAME CHAMBER WHERE A GIANT, BLACK-COWLED FIGURE WAITED EAGERLY...

LET GO! DON'T YOU DARE HARM HER!

BRING THEM TO ME...AND BEGONE! THEIR HOUR OF DEATH IS AT HAND!

ONE OF THE HEADLESS SLAVES RELEASED HIS HOLD ON MORELY. WITH ONE SPRING THE AMERICAN PULLED OUT HIS SWORD ...AND CHARGED THE FIGURE IN BLACK!

YOU'RE NOT GOING TO DO THE SAME ACT OF EVIL AGAIN! LADY ANN HAS HAD ENOUGH TORTURE!

FOOL! SHE MUST PLAY OUT HER PART FOR ALL ETERNITY AS MUST I !

THE SOUNDS OF THAT TREMENDOUS STRUGGLE REVERBERATED THROUGHOUT THE HALLS OF THE CASTLE... THEN, BILL MADE HIS MOVE...

BACK TO WHATEVER HELL YOU CAME FROM, MONSTER! THIS IS THE TALISMAN THAT WILL DAMN YOU!

AN OLIVE BRANCH! YA-AAAAAAAH-H! DO NOT HOLD IT BEFORE MY GAZE! NO! NO!

I THOUGHT SO! YOU'RE THE BLACK DUKE OF MALBA...THE EVIL WRETCH THAT PUT ALL THE PEOPLE OF THIS CASTLE TO THE SWORD! OFF WITH YOUR HELMET SO THAT I MAY SEE YOUR FACE!

FOOL!! FOOL!! DO NOT UNCLOAK ME!

YES...I AM DEATH!! THE SOUL OF THE EVIL MALBA RESIDES WITHIN ME IN COMPOSITE WITH OTHER SINNERS! THE HEADLESS ONES WERE THOSE WHOM MALBA HAD CONQUERED IN COMBAT! THEY MUST SERVE HIM UNTIL THE END OF TIME!... AS HE HIMSELF MUST SERVE ME! GO NOW...AND FORGET! THE CURSE OF MORO CASTLE HAS ENDED!

YOU SHALL FORGET IN TIME! FAREWELL, BILL MORELY...

WHHEEEEEEEOOOO

A BLINDING FLASH OF LIGHT...A PINWHEELING CIRCLE INCREASING TO UNIVERSAL LUMINESCENCE... THEN BLACKNESS! AND WHEN NEXT BILL MORELY AWOKE, HE WAS OUTSIDE MORO CASTLE, HIS FACE CRADLED IN A BEAUTIFUL GIRL'S LAP!

IT'S MORNING! I...WH-WHAT HAPPENED? W-WHO ARE YOU!

I WAS DRIVING TO THE CASTLE WHEN I SAW YOU LYING HERE! YOU WERE IN DELIRIUM! ARE YOU HURT?

NO! I-I MUST HAVE HAD A NIGHTMARE... AND WALKED OUT OF MY OWN HOUSE... BUT...YOUR FACE...IT'S THAT OF LADY ANN!

LADY ANN? STRANGE YOU SHOULD SAY THAT! SHE HAPPENS TO BE MY FAR ANCESTOR! I'M THE NEW OWNER OF THIS CASTLE... LINDA POLERA... BUT HOW DID YOU KNOW?

NEVER MIND! IT DOESN'T MATTER REALLY! I'M YOUR NEIGHBOR ACROSS THE WAY! I'M SURE WE'RE GOING TO SEE A GREAT DEAL OF EACH OTHER...BUT I WONDER WHERE I GOT THE NAME OF LADY ANN? I WONDER?....

THE END

WE KNOW THAT THE AIR AND SEA AND SOLID LAND ABOUND IN A VARIETY OF CREATURES-- BUT WHO CAN TELL WHAT HIDEOUS THINGS DWELL DEEP IN THE PUTRID OOZE OF THE SWAMP-LAND? BE CAREFUL-- FOR SOME TIME WHEN YOU ARE ON THE EDGE OF SOME DESOLATE MIRE YOU MAY MEET...

THE SWAMP MONSTER!

BUCK QUENTIN AND SAM MARBLE WERE DEEP IN THE AMAZON SWAMP COUNTRY, SEEKING OIL...

WE WANT YOU TO DREDGE THE BOTTOM OF THE NORTH SIDE OF THE LAKE, PEDRO! FROM WHAT WE HEARD, THAT MUD IS RICH IN OIL DEPOSITS!

NO...NO...SENOR! NOT NEAR THE BLACK SWAMP!

A TERRIBLE MONSTER SLUMBERS IN THE BLACK SWAMP! THEY WHO GO NEAR THERE NEVER RETURN!

1

FELIPE PADDLED FURIOUSLY TO REACH HIS FATHER, AND WHEN HE NEARED THE DREADED BLACK SWAMP...

FATHER! COME BACK! I AM FREE!

BUT EVEN AS PEDRO TURNED, A QUIVERING MASS OF MUCK BILLOWED UPWARD, AND...

FATHER! BEHIND YOU! AAAHHH!

THE FIENDS! THEY SENT MY FATHER TO THE MONSTER!

ARRGHRRR

FATHER! YOU... YOU LET THIS HAPPEN TO SAVE MY LIFE!

HIS HIDEOUS HUNGER SATED, THE MONSTER SUNK BENEATH THE MARSH ONCE MORE, WHILE FELIPE WATCHED... UNAWARE OF THE CHANGE THE HORROR HAD WROUGHT ON HIM!

I MUST KILL THEM! IT IS NOT VENGEANCE ENOUGH... BUT IT IS THE LEAST I CAN DO!

3

FELIPE SLUNK BACK TO CAMP, AND...

THE GUNS ARE NOT HERE... THEY ARE IN *THAT* CASE... LOCKED! HOW CAN I KILL THEM WITHOUT A GUN?

SUDDENLY...

PEDRO! WHAT ARE YOU DOING HERE? DID YOU GET THE MUD SAMPLES?

WH-WHAT? HE...HE CALLED ME BY MY FATHER'S NAME! THAT IS STRANGE!

MY FACE... MY HAIR... LIKE MY FATHER'S! THE TERROR OF WATCHING...IT..IT AGED ME! HE WAS RIGHT, MY FATHER, PEDRO... THE GODS HAVE FOUND A WAY TO REPAY THEM!

YES, SENOR, I HAVE THE SAMPLE! ONE MOMENT, AND I WILL BRING IT TO YOU!

SEE? I TOLD YOU THERE WAS NOTHING BUT SUPERSTITIOUS NONSENSE IN THAT STORY OF A MONSTER!

OUTSIDE... THIS MUCK FROM THE WATER'S EDGE... I WILL DRENCH IT WITH OIL, AND THEN WE WILL SEE HOW SILLY THE MONSTER IS!

SOON... WHEW! RICHEST DEPOSIT I'VE EVER SEEN! WHERE IS THAT PEDRO? WE'LL GET HIM TO PADDLE US OVER AT ONCE SO WE CAN STAKE A CLAIM!

4

5 The End

TABOO

BECAUSE KINGS WERE CONSIDERED SACRED PEOPLE YEARS AGO, IT WAS TABOO TO TOUCH THEM, AND KING TIENG-TSONG-TAI-OANG SUFFERED BY THE DECREE AS HE WASTED AWAY TO DEATH FROM A TUMOR ON HIS BACK...NO ONE DARED TOUCH HIM!

DURING THE DARK AGES, IT WAS TABOO FOR *VISITORS* TO COME INTO THE PRESENCE OF TARTAR KHAN UNLESS THEY PASSED THROUGH TWO GREAT FIRES!

WARRIORS TABOOED!

AMONG SOME OF OUR INDIAN TRIBES, IT WAS TABOO FOR A YOUNG WARRIOR IN HIS FIRST CAMPAIGN TO SCRATCH HIS HEAD OR ANY PART OF HIS BODY. HIS TABOOED FINGERS WERE CONSIDERED POLLUTED!

THE ISLAND OF TIMOR INFLICTS A TABOO ON THE VICTORIOUS WARRIOR. THE LEADER OF A TRIUMPHANT EXPEDITION, BRINGING BACK THE HEADS OF THEIR ENEMIES, MUST LIVE IN SECLUSION FOR TWO MONTHS TO BE CLEANSED OF THE BATTLE DEMONS.

WHEN THE FIJIANS BURIED A MAN ALIVE, AS WAS THEIR CUSTOM, THEY WOULD CAUSE A LOATHESOME TUMULT WITH SHOUTS, TRUMPET-SHELLS AND DRUM-BEATS TO FRIGHTEN AWAY THE GHOST.

TABOOED BLOOD

IT WAS A COMMON RULE THAT THE BLOOD OF A KING SHALL NOT BE SHED. THUS, WHEN THE KUBLAI KHAN DEFEATED NAYAN, HIS UNCLE, HE PUT HIM TO DEATH BY HAVING HIM WRAPT IN A CARPET AND TOSSED AND TWISTED...TILL THE END!

MARCO POLO TOLD OF A HORRIBLE PRACTICE OF ANCIENT PEKING. IF A PERSON WAS FOUND GUILTY OF A CRIME, HE WAS BEATEN UNMERCIFULLY WITH A STICK UNTIL HE DIED, AND THIS WAS NOT CONSIDERED EVIL-- FOR THEY DID NOT SHED BLOOD!

MANY PEOPLE OF WEST AFRICA COVER OR STAMP OUT ANY OF THEIR BLOOD THAT HAS FALLEN SO THAT MAGICIANS CANNOT GET HOLD OF IT TO USE IT IN EVIL WAYS.

The SNOW BEASTS

The butler closed the door of the reading room of the Explorer's Club. Inside, ten world-famous travelers settled deeper in their chairs. The shadows of twilight cautiously crept through the huge swinging windows.

"Well, Johnson, go ahead. We're all here."

Marlon Johnson, the man who had explored the whole of Africa and Tibet, crushed out his cigarette and wet his lips.

"Gentlemen, take a firm grip on your chairs. What I am about to tell you will challenge your imagination and probably force you to call me insane. But, this story is true. It's true! TRUE!"

"Johnson! Easy! We know you've been under a terrific strain but you must try to control yourself."

The almost hysterical explorer brushed the ring of perspiration from his forehead. Trembling, he lit a cigarette.

"Of-of course, gentlemen! I'm sorry. I'll be all right.

"It all happened a year ago this month. I had just returned from a safari into Africa. We had brought back some wonderful animal specimens and our spirits were running high. Mine were probably running very high. A short while later, I was contacted by a Mr. Crowley. He was known for his work in photography and wanted me to accompany him into the wilds of Tibet. It seems ... it seems he had heard of a lost race of people who lived in the storm-swept mountains of that country.

"This race was supposedly to have been driven to the mountains by Ghengis Khan's soldiers and isolated there. Then, because of the geographical conditions, their bodies changed to adapt themselves to extreme cold and driving snows.

"So it is that the natives of Tibet had claimed to have seen hairy giants in the passes of the mountains. One man claimed that this hair or fur was red and extremely long. Others said these creatures looked like bears standing upright. At any rate, I was convinced that the expedition would be exciting enough to warrant my going with it."

By now, Johnson had again reached a highly nervous state. Though his voice seemed steady, his hands were trembling and fumbling with the sides of his chair.

Once more, the gathered men calmed him down. A hurried drink of brandy allowed him to continue.

"We made all the necessary arrangements and, three weeks after Crowley had contacted me, we were on our way to Tibet!

"I will not burden you with all the details of the trip. I will, instead, bring you to the point where we met the monsters."

"Met the monsters!"

"You mean they actually do exist!"

"Come now, old boy, we've been around a bit ourselves!"

"Stop! We did meet the monsters of the snow!"

These last words of Johnson jolted the others into a tense silence. The room seemed to freeze with tension.

"We met them one savage afternoon. The elements had apparently waited for that time to unleash their power.

"Well, as we struggled up a slope, our lead guide gave a sudden start and ran back down to us. All he could do was point!

"When we saw what he was pointing at, our sanity began to tear apart ... to shred into wild thoughts. Standing there above us, framed in the swirling torrents of snow, was a snow monster!"

Johnson stopped his narrative and glared at the men about him. Their faces, intent enough, registered obvious doubt.

"Do you mean to tell us that you actually saw the beast or whatever it was?"

"You realize, Johnson, that what you are saying is in effect that such a race of people does exist."

"But I did! Whatever this thing was, it had long red hair and teeth like a wolf's. It stood there grinning at us and then ... and then it attacked!

"With a savage growl it hurled itself upon us and we had to meet it hand to hand! We fought wildly in the snow for what seemed hours.

"All three of our guides and Crowley were killed. I must have collapsed and appeared dead to it for it left me alone. It must have been some time after that the search party found me."

"But tell us, Johnson, what proof have you that this race exists or that this monster you met exists? You have no pictures."

Johnson rose.

"No gentlemen, I have no pictures but neither do I have a right arm!"

Johnson faced sideways to the others and exposed the stump of what had been his right arm. It had been horribly torn off at the shoulder,

The BRIDE of the CRAB

She got what she wanted... but she didn't know the price she'd have to pay... for below her, in the thick slime of a strange undersea world, they lurked... watching and waiting for her.

The ancient Donder Mansion was thick with gloom as old Silas Donder lay on his deathbed...

Goodbye, Donald, my son. I feel the hand of death on me. After tonight, you will never see me again.

No, no! Don't say that, Dad!

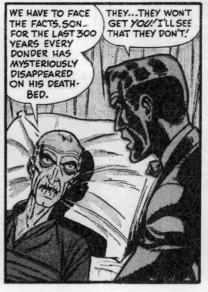

We have to face the facts, son.. for the last 300 years every Donder has mysteriously disappeared on his death-bed.

They...they won't get you! I'll see that they don't!

Whoever or whatever it is that snatches the Donders from their deathbeds...I...I'll see that you're safe from it!

1

MAYBE, SON, BUT I FEEL THAT YOU'LL NEVER SEE ME AGAIN! BEFORE I BID YOU FAREWELL, THERE IS A SECRET I MUST IMPART TO YOU. BELOW THE CELLAR IS A SUBTERRANEAN PASSAGE THAT LEADS TO THE SEA...

...AT HIGH TIDE IT IS FLOODED, BUT AT LOW TIDE IT LEADS TO THE VERY MOUTH OF THE WATERS. THERE, YOU WILL FIND STRANGE AND RICH TREASURES...AS MUCH AS YOU WANT! I DON'T KNOW WHY, BUT IT HAS ALWAYS BEEN SO.

ALL THAT NIGHT, YOUNG DONALD SAT AT HIS FATHER'S DOOR...

THEY WON'T GET HIM...THEY WON'T!

HOWEVER, TOWARD MORNING, HE MOMENTARILY FELL ASLEEP AND WHEN HE AWOKE...

HE...HE'S GONE! THEY...THEY CAN'T HAVE TAKEN HIM FAR. I...I'VE ONLY BEEN ASLEEP A FEW MINUTES!

TRACKS! FOOTPRINTS OF STRANGE BEASTS...AND THAT SLIME, AND SEAWEED! WH-WHAT ARE THEY? WH-WHERE HAVE THEY TAKEN HIM!

DONALD FOLLOWED THE TRACKS... THROUGH THE HOUSE, DOWN THE CELLAR, AND FINALLY...

THEY...THEY LEAD TO THE VERY PASSAGEWAY DAD TOLD ME ABOUT...BELOW THE HOUSE, AND OUT TO THE SEA! MAYBE I...I'M NOT TOO LATE!

2

SUDDENLY... THOSE HORRIBLE CREATURES! THEY... THEY'RE CARRYING DAD INTO THE SEA! *WHY?*

DONALD! GO BACK... GO BACK!

LET HIM GO! LET HIM GO!

AS THE TERRIBLY COLD CLAW-LIKE HAND GRIPPED HIM, YOUNG DONDER FAINTED!

HIS CLAW... LIKE COLD STEEL... THE CHILL OF DEATH RUNNING THROUGH MY BODY. I...I... *AAAAH...*

AND WHEN HE REGAINED CONSCIOUSNESS...

DAD! HELP! HELP! COME QUICK!

HIS TERROR-CHARGED VOICE ECHOED THROUGH THE LONELY WALLS, AND...

MASTER DONALD! WHAT IS IT?

THEY--THEY TOOK HIM... HORRIBLE CREATURES... SNATCHED MY FATHER FROM HIS DEATHBED AND TOOK HIM BELOW THE SEA.

THOSE TRACKS...IT...IT MUST BE TRUE! WHAT STRANGE AND TERRIBLE CURSE HANGS OVER THIS HOUSE?

TAKE ME AWAY! TAKE ME AWAY! I NEVER WANT TO SEE DONDER MANOR AGAIN!

DONALD GRADUALLY RECOVERED, AND FOR TWO YEARS DONDER MANOR AND ITS GRIM SECRETS WERE CLOSED TO THE WORLD...

AND THEN DONALD FELL IN LOVE. SHE WAS BEAUTIFUL....BUT SHREWD AND CALCULATING...

PLEASE, MONA ...WON'T YOU MARRY ME?

I'M PERFECTLY WILLING...BUT I HAVE EXPENSIVE TASTES, AND UNLESS MY HUSBAND CAN BUY ME WHATEVER I WANT, *NEITHER* OF US WILL BE VERY HAPPY.

AND IF I GET MONEY...LOTS OF IT...YOU WILL?

OF COURSE, DARLING. *IF.*

I'VE NEVER TOLD YOU BEFORE...BECAUSE I...I WAS AFRAID TO. THERE'S SUPPOSED TO BE A VERITABLE TREASURE BENEATH MY ANCESTRAL HOME, BUT THERE ARE THINGS THERE ...SO DREADFUL...

OLD WIVES TALES. I'LL GO WITH YOU-- AND SHOW YOU THERE'S NOTHING TO BE AFRAID OF.

SOME TIME LATER, DEEP UNDER THE DONDER MANSE...

IT...IT WAS HERE THAT I SAW THEM! ONE OF THEM TOUCHED ME AND THE COLD...

THE FOOL! HE'S OUT OF HIS MIND! IF I DIDN'T KNOW THAT THE DONDERS ALWAYS HAD MORE MONEY THAN THEY COULD USE, I'D NEVER HAVE COME WITH HIM!

LOOK! THE TREASURE! JUST AS MY FATHER TOLD ME!

A...A FORTUNE IN GEMS AND GOLD! IF ONLY I COULD HAVE IT FOR MYSELF...WITHOUT BEING TIED TO THAT WEAK-WITTED, SPINELESS FOOL THE REST OF MY LIFE!

HERE, MONA...ALL OF IT FOR YOU! YOU...YOU'LL KEEP YOUR PROMISE?

YES! YES! OF COURSE!

SUDDENLY...

AGGGHH!

4

NEVER MIND THE TREASURE! MY HEAD ...HELP ME!

HAVE TO PICK THEM UP BEFORE THE TIDE FLOODS THE PASSAGEWAY. IT--IT'S RISING ALREADY!

MONA! DON'T LEAVE ME! I...I'M DYING! THEY...THEY'LL GET ME!

NONSENSE! THERE ARE NO HORRIBLE CREATURES! IT'S JUST YOUR SICK IMAGINATION!

IF HE DIES BEFORE I MARRY HIM, THE TREASURE WON'T BE MINE, BUT THIS WAY...EVERYTHING I'VE ALWAYS WANTED!

MOMENTS LATER, AS DONALD STRUGGLED WITH HIS LAST BREATHS...

THEY...THEY'VE COME FOR ME...AS THEY'VE ALWAYS COME FOR THE DONDERS!

DO NOT BE AFRAID, DONALD DONDER! WE ARE HERE TO HELP YOU! THREE HUNDRED YEARS AGO, ONE OF YOUR ANCESTORS DISCOVERED THIS SERUM WHICH CONTAINS THE SECRET OF IMMORTAL LIFE, AND SINCE THEN, WHENEVER A DONDER HAS BEEN ABOUT TO DIE...

...WE GIVE HIM THE GIFT OF YEARS WITHOUT END. THE SERUM WILL CHANGE YOU...AS WE HAVE BEEN CHANGED...AND BENEATH THE SEA, YOU WILL LIVE FOREVER IN YOUR NEW SHAPE!

THOSE TREASURES YOU SAW...WE DREDGED THEM FROM THE LIMITLESS WEALTH THAT LIES BENEATH THE SEA...AND GAVE THEM TO OUR PEOPLE! SOON, YOU WILL SEE FOR YOURSELF OUR LAND BELOW THE WATER!

COME. YOU ARE READY.

ETERNAL LIFE BENEATH THE SEA.. IT WILL BE GOOD.. BUT STILL....I...I WANT...MONA. SHE PROMISED.

5

SOME WEEKS LATER, IN THE MOST EXPENSIVE CABIN OF AN OCEAN LINER...

EVERYTHING I WANTED...AND WITHOUT BEING SHACKLED TO THAT FOOL WITH HIS RIDICULOUS FANTASIES OF HORRIBLE CREATURES!

AT THAT INSTANT... THOSE STRANGE SCRABBLING SOUNDS...LIKE CLAWS SCRATCHING AT MY DOOR..WH-WHAT CAN THEY BE?

NO! NO! EEEHHH! HELP!

NOW YOU SEE...THE CREATURES I SPOKE OF...THEY...THEY EXIST!

IT...IT'S DONALD'S VOICE! HIS FACE! TH-THAT MONSTROUS THING IS DONALD!

YES...NOW I AM ONE OF THEM ...AND SO WILL YOU BE, SOON.

DONALD! PLEASE! I'M SORRY! LET ME GO! LET ME GO!

THE CRAB-LIKE CREATURE SLITHERED SILENTLY TO THE EDGE OF THE DECK, AND CRAWLED DOWN THE SIDE OF THE BOAT, CLUTCHING HIS PREY..HIS BRIDE!

DON'T YOU REMEMBER YOUR PROMISE? NOW YOU CAN KEEP IT...FOREVER!

THE END

6

THE FRUIT OF DEATH!

FOR YEARS THE TREE HAD BEEN FRUIT-LESS--A BLEAK AND BARREN WOODEN SKELETON STRETCH-ING GNARLED AND EMPTY BRANCHES TOWARD THE SKY-- UNTIL SUDDENLY IT BLOSSOMED FORTH AND BORE...

RAFE DESTER AND HIS WIFE SARA SCRAPED A MEAGRE LIVING FROM THE POOR AND SANDY SOIL OF THEIR BACK COUNTRY FARM...

I DON'T KNOW WHY I MARRIED YOU. THERE ISN'T ENOUGH ON THIS FARM TO KEEP SKIN AND BONES TOGETHER.

ENOUGH TO KEEP YOUR TONGUE RATTLIN' IN YOUR HEAD AS USUAL. DON'T YOU NEVER DO NOTHIN' BUT COMPLAIN?

THE BITTER ACID THAT ATE INTO THE SOIL SEEMED TO SEETHE IN THEIR SOULS, TOO!

I'D LEAVE YOU IN AN INSTANT IF I HAD SOMEWHERE ELSE TO GO!

AND I'D CHUCK YOU OUT EVEN FASTER IF I DIDN'T HAVE TO SUPPORT YOU AFTER-WARD!

THE DESTERS ARGUED ABOUT EVERYTHING... BUT THEY ARGUED MOST ABOUT *THE TREE!*

HMMPH! THE ONLY DECENT PIECE OF SOIL ON THE WHOLE FARM... AND YOU WASTE IT ON THAT TREE!

IT'S NOT WASTED! ONE DAY IT WILL BEAR FRUIT--SWEET AND DELICIOUS FRUIT!

ALL MY LIFE I'VE DREAMED OF THE DAY... WHEN I CAN STRETCH OUT MY HAND AND HAVE ALL THE FRESH FRUIT I WANT!

YAH! YOU DREAM... AND MEANWHILE WE STARVE WHILE IT'S UGLY, TWISTED ROOTS DRAIN THE GOOD SOIL DRY! ONE DAY I'LL CHOP IT DOWN!

YOU DO THAT, AND I... I'LL KILL YOU!

SARA WAS AFRAID TO CARRY OUT HER THREAT UNTIL...

BLIGHT RUINED THE WHOLE POTATO CROP! WE'LL HAVE PRACTICALLY NOTHIN' TO EAT UNLESS WE USE THAT RICH SOIL TO PLANT ON! IT'S TIME THAT USELESS TREE CAME DOWN... *IT HAS TO!*

I'LL DO IT! *NOW*-- WHILE HE'S AWAY!

BARELY HAD THE AXE BITTEN INTO THE BARK WHEN...

THE TREE! SHE'S CHOPPIN' DOWN THE TREE!

2

RAFE'S LIMP BODY FELL TO THE GROUND AND PALE GHOULISH HANDS SCRABBLED IN THE EARTH, DIGGING A SHALLOW GRAVE!

RAFE'S BODY WAS LAID NEXT TO THE BLEACHED BONES MOULDERING AT THE BASE OF THE TREE...

BUT NEXT SPRING, THE TREE FINALLY BORE FRUIT...

IN EARLY SUMMER, THE WITHERED BLOOMS FELL TO THE GROUND, CRISP AND FADED, STIRRED BY THE RESTLESS WINDS...

THE END

5

Finale of DEATH

He let the corpse of the Indian magician slide from his arms. Clutched tightly in his right hand, was a piece of paper on which was written the most fabulous secret ever known to man.

"I-I can go into a person's mind at will."

The words were half mumbled-half whispered. Hugo Dobbs was caught in a void of shock. The world-renowned magician, Aga Pasha, had just died leaving him in possession of a secret men would kill for!

Hugo Dobbs now had the power of entering another person's mind and actually follow every thought in that person's mind. He could, at all times, know what anyone was thinking and he could accomplish this feat even though his subject was thousands of miles away!

The days passed. Dobbs needed time to think ...to think about what he would do with this power. Then, he decided!

"I'll call together all of the leading scientists. I'll demonstrate what I can do. I'll let them supply a solution as they are the only ones who could fully comprehend such a thing as this."

When the appointed night of the gathering came, Hugo Dobbs could barely stand. What he would have to say might thrust humanity before the threshold of a mental revolution. Perhaps other dimensions could be found. Perhaps...

"They're ready, sir!"

Dobbs was snapped out of his thought.

"Yes, y-yes!"

After a half hour, the assembled men, who comprised the leading scientific minds of the world, were fully aware of the power Dobbs held. Their faces drained to a pale white and their hands began to tremble. Finally, one of them spoke:

"Mr. Dobbs, now that you have informed us of your power, it is necessary that we witness a demonstration. As you know, every scientific discovery must be proved in demonstration."

"Of course! Of course!"

Dobbs looked about the room for a subject. He noticed a strange looking man in the corner and chose him.

The man walked forward as if death held him by the ankles. Dobbs seated him and, then, began!

"I will now enter your mind! I will be able to go into every cell of your mind and explore them minutely."

"There! I've done it! I'm in his mind! Here! I'll walk down this corridor. Look at those cells ...as if I were in some prison. The odor is sickening! What!!!

"Who are you? Keep away from me!

"I must run from it! Oh no! There are more coming at me from behind!

Eeeeeyyyaaaahhhh! That's a fire to my left. My skin is blistering. I must run!

"Stop! Stop clawing at me! My eyes! My eyes!

"What kind of a place is this! Is this the human mind? Monsters? Monsters? Fires! Fires!

"Aiieehhh! Now I'm stuck in this slime. I can't move. Noooo! Those things hanging over my head. They're human bodies and the heads have been cut off. I'M STUCK IN THEIR BLOOD!

"Let me out! Let me out! Ahaaaaa! Ha! Ha! Haaaaaa!

"Please let me out! Please!"

"Somebody get some water. Mr. Dobbs has fainted!"

As the scientists rushed to Dobbs, the rear door smashed open and armed police appeared.

"There he is! Let's get him!"

They dragged away the man whom Hugo Dobbs was using for a subject.

One of the scientists stepped forward and grabbed a policeman by the arm.

"What is the meaning of this, officer!"

"That's an easy one! That guy we're hauling out of here just escaped from the nut house. He's Rocky Taylor, the mad killer! He must have sneaked in here somehow!"

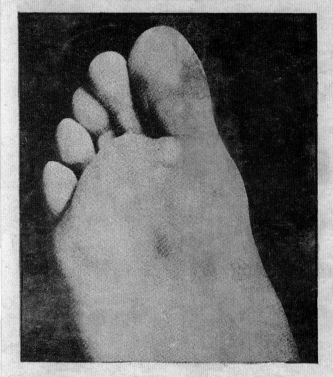

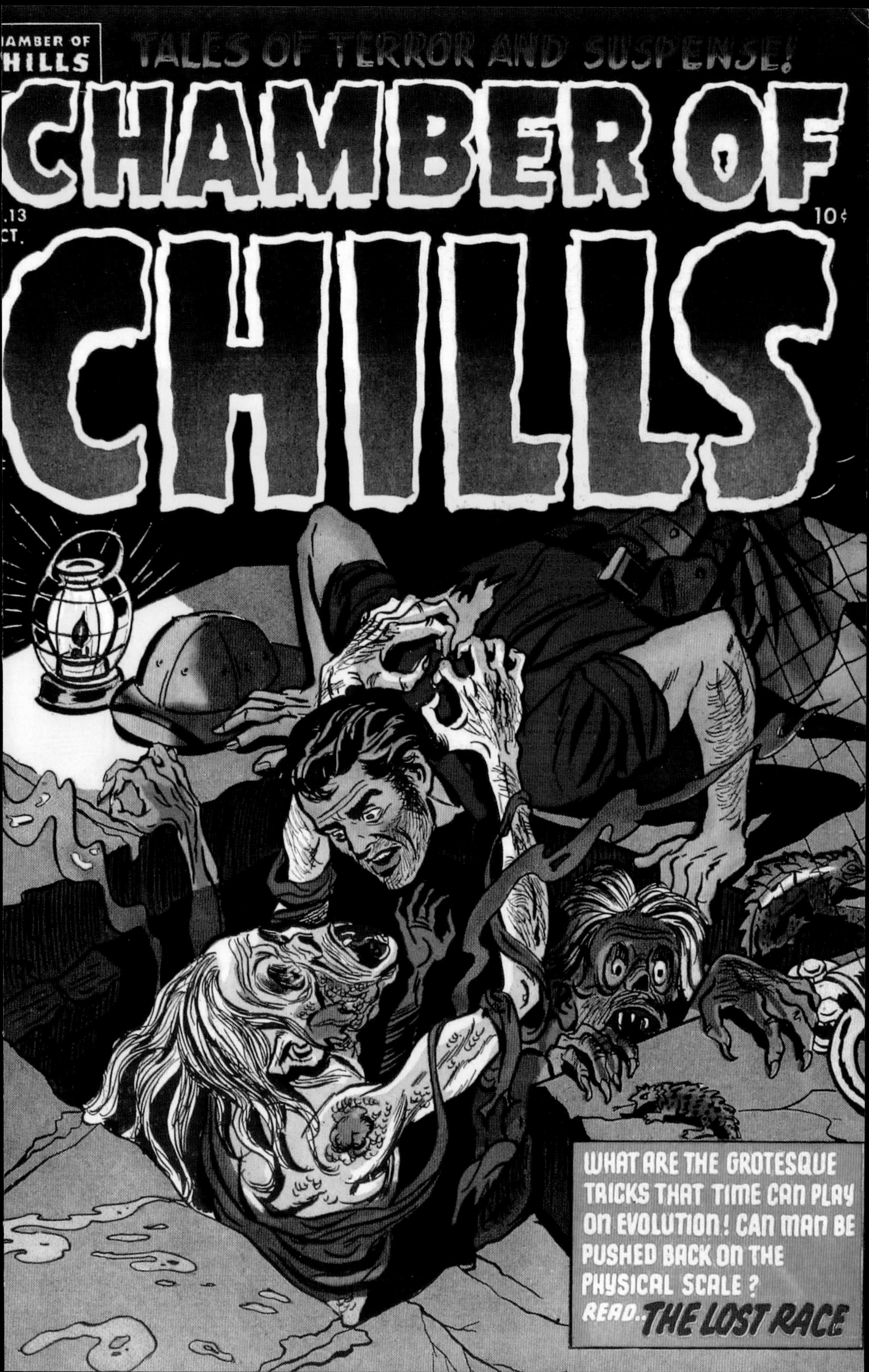

CHAMBER OF CHILLS
TALES OF TERROR AND SUSPENSE!
CHAMBER OF CHILLS
.13
CT.
10¢
WHAT ARE THE GROTESQUE TRICKS THAT TIME CAN PLAY ON EVOLUTION! CAN MAN BE PUSHED BACK ON THE PHYSICAL SCALE?
READ..THE LOST RACE

You have come from the outer world . . . you have crossed the scorching infernos . . . you have entered the realm of mystery . . . you have arrived at the CHAMBER OF CHILLS!

This is the world of infinite horror, where evil runs berserk, where Satan smiles a pitiless smile, where man is caught and held!

Mortals dare entice the demons of these depths and become entangled in the tentacles of terror, the violence of evil and the eerie roads of the unknown!

The walls move closer . . . closer . . . closer and all exits are closed from the CHAMBER OF CHILLS!

For here is the home of horror . . . the manse of madness . . . the store-house of suspense . . . the battlefield of the weird!

Midnight spills its inky slime and the carpet of mystery is spread. Up from the earth come the ghouls that dwell in its core . . . in from the unknown swoop the creatures that rule in that realm . . . all come together and join in the tales of terror that make the CHAMBER OF CHILLS!

Cast your eyes on these pages that drip with suspense . . . the weird . . . the unusual. Feel your pulse quicken . . . your spine tingle! Drink in the greatest mixture of stories ever assembled . . . Feast on this world of fear . . . Read the . . .

CHAMBER OF CHILLS!

THE GRUESOME GUILLOTINE SYMBOLIZES THE VIOLENCE AND DEATH THAT IS ASSOCIATED WITH THE HISTORIC FRENCH REVOLUTION! AND THE MOST FEARED EXECUTIONER OF THEM ALL WAS THE...

MAN IN THE HOOD!

NO! I'VE KILLED YOU ALL!

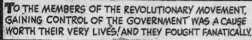

TO THE MEMBERS OF THE REVOLUTIONARY MOVEMENT, GAINING CONTROL OF THE GOVERNMENT WAS A CAUSE WORTH THEIR VERY LIVES! AND THEY FOUGHT FANATICALLY.

DEATH TO THE KING AND HIS FOLLOWERS!

AGGGRRRAAA!

AIIIIEEEE! THE REVOLUTIONARIES!

1

AND THE REIGN OF TERROR IS WELL NAMED!

AGGGGRRRAAAA!

MORE! MORE!

WHACK

LONG LIVE THE KING!

ONE LESS OF ROYALIST SWINE! HA-HA!

SPARE ME-- PLEASE!

DEATH! DEATH! THE KING'S HEAD AWAITS US! HA-HA!

AND IN THE REVOLUTIONARIES' PRISON NEARBY...OTHER ROYALISTS AWAIT THE GRIM CALL TO THE BLOOD-STAINED GUILLOTINE AND ITS FIENDISH OPERATOR!

THIS WAITING! WHY DON'T THEY KILL US AND GET IT OVER WITH!

BLAME THE GUILLOTINE FOR BEING ABLE TO ACCOMMODATE BUT ONE HEAD AT A TIME!

I...I...FEEL FAINT! HOW CAN YOU BE SO CALM!

I GUESS THIS RUNS IN MY FAMILY! MY FATHER DIED BY THE GUILLOTINE ALSO!

THE MADDENED EXECUTIONER FLEES HYSTERICALLY THROUGH THE DARKENED CORRIDORS OF THE REVOLUTIONARY PRISON! BUT THE HIDEOUS VISIONS PURSUE RELENTLESSLY!

GO BACK! YOU'RE DEAD, I SAY! DEAD!

AIEEEE! TRAPPED!

I KNOW WHO YOU ARE, HIGH EXECUTIONER!

NO! NO--! I.....

YES--!

ALL RIGHT. THEN YOU KNOW! I AM YOUR FATHER!

THERE! SEE ME AS I AM!

SACRE BLEU! HIS HEAD!

HAVING REVEALED THE BLOOD-CURDLING TRUTH, THE INFAMOUS MAN IN THE HOOD CRUMPLES TO THE GROUND...

I KILLED HIM AND HE KILLED ME! WILL MAN EVER KNOW PEACE!?

THE END.   6

THE LOST RACE!

Deep beneath the surface of the earth, hidden in loathesome pits and fetid crevices are the creatures for whom time moves backward! Beware! For some day they will crawl from their foul homes...and the world will be ruled by...

IT WON'T BE LONG, SOON WE WILL COME OUT,...SOON YOU WILL SEE US IN THE STREETS! SOON *WE* WILL BE THE *MASTERS* OF THE *EARTH!*

I AM PROFESSOR HENRY PEYTON. BEFORE I LEARNED THE TRUTH, I WAS SURE OF MY IDEAS. I REMEMBER HOW I LECTURED TO MY CLASSES...

EVOLUTION IS THE PROCESS OF CHANGE BY WHICH NATURE DEVELOPS MORE AND MORE PERFECT BEINGS!

NATURE IS ALWAYS EXPERIMENTING...IMPROVING CERTAIN SPECIES, DISCARDING OTHERS.

AEONS AGO, BEFORE MAN APPEARED ON THE WORLD, CREATURES LIKE THESE MAY HAVE SWARMED OVER THE EARTH...

BUT NATURE ELIMINATED THEM ...ALWAYS IMPROVING THE SPECIES... ALWAYS MOVING FORWARD.

ARE YOU SURE, PROFESSOR PEYTON? ISN'T IT POSSIBLE FOR EVOLUTION TO GO *BACKWARDS*?

PREPOSTEROUS! THE WHOLE HISTORY OF EVOLUTION PROVES... ER...PROVES THAT COULDN'T HAPPEN!

AND YET...THOSE BONES DUG UP IN AFRICA ...I WONDER!

I RECALLED THAT BAFFLING DISCOVERY MADE YEARS AGO IN THE HEART OF AFRICA...

IT'S INCREDIBLE! NO CREATURE LIKE IT IS KNOWN TO HAVE EXISTED!

WHAT MYSTIFIES ME IS THAT THOSE BONES ARE ONLY A FEW HUNDRED YEARS OLD!

IS IT POSSIBLE THAT EVOLUTION IS MOVING BACKWARD FOR SOME RACE LOST IN THE PRIMITIVE JUNGLES OF AFRICA? I...I *MUST* FIND OUT!

I HAD A LEAVE COMING TO ME, AND EMBARKED FOR AFRICA, WHERE...

WE CAMP HERE!

THE VERY SPOT WHERE CARRUTHERS DUG UP THOSE BONES. I'LL START DIGGING TOMORROW!

I SPENT THAT DAY IN STUDY, AND WHEN I INSPECTED THE PROGRESS THE NATIVES HAD MADE IN DIGGING...

HMMM... STRANGE ODOR COMING FROM THE PIT... DANK AND BITTER... WONDER WHAT HAPPENED TO THE NATIVES.

YOU THERE! CHIEF TULA! WHERE ARE THE OTHERS?

THEY RUN AWAY! SAY EVIL SPIRITS DWELL UNDERGROUND!

FOG OF DEATH RISES FROM EARTH! RUN... RUN... BEFORE IT KILLS YOU!

NONSENSE! IT'S JUST SOME KIND OF NATURAL GAS! COME BACK! COME BACK!

HMMPH... CAN'T DO MUCH ALONE. I'LL TAKE A LAST LOOK AND THEN GO BACK TO THE VILLAGE. GUESS I'LL NEED A NEW BATCH OF DIGGERS!

I LOOKED DOWN THAT PIT... AND GASPED IN SHEER HORROR, CLAMMY FINGERS OF TERROR TRICKLING DOWN MY SPINE!

THOSE CREATURES! THEY... THEY'RE LIKE THE SKELETON... ONLY COVERED WITH FLESH... ROTTING FLESH!

3

HORRIBLE HANDS... HAIRY AND OOZING WITH SLIME REACHED OUT AND CLUTCHED ME TIGHTLY!

AAAGHH

THEY CARRIED ME BELOW...TO THE FETID, TWISTING HONEYCOMB OF CAVERNS THEY INHABITED...

THAT TERRIBLE GAS...IT...IT'S CHOKING ME...SEEPING INTO EVERY PORE OF MY BODY!

I WAS THROWN INTO A CORNER, AND OTHERS CAME, PRODDING ME CURIOUSLY...

THEY...THEY'RE PART HUMAN...PART BEAST. THEY MUST HAVE BEEN TRAPPED UNDERGROUND...AND THE STRANGE ATMOSPHERE HERE HAS MADE THEM EVOLVE BACKWARDS... INTO GHASTLY CREATURES THAT INHABITED THE EARTH EONS AGO!

THEY...THEY'RE GOING TO KILL ME...EAT ME...AS IF *I* WAS AN ANIMAL!

MUST DO SOMETHING...QUICK... A MATCH! IGNITE THE GAS THAT'S PART OF THE AIR THEY BREATHE! IT MAY BLOW UP THE WHOLE CAVERN...BUT WHAT HAVE I TO LOSE?

THAT'S SCARED THEM! NOW IF I CAN ONLY GET OUT WHILE THEY'RE STILL TERRIFIED...

4

I TRIED TO RUN... BUT MY PATH WAS BLOCKED BY THOUSANDS OF GROTESQUE BODIES... KNEELING IN OBEISANCE!

THAT FLAMING GAS... THEY THINK I'M A GOD... THEY... THEY... WORSHIP ME... WON'T LET ME GO! I... I CAN'T GET PAST THEM... BUT AT LEAST THEY WON'T HARM ME!

THEY WERE SLAVES TO ME, AND BOWED REVERENTLY WHENEVER THEY SAW ME, BUT...

NIGHT AND DAY THEY GUARD THE ENTRANCE TO THAT PIT... FOR FEAR I'LL LEAVE THEM. I'M DOOMED TO SPEND THE REST OF MY LIFE IN THIS RANK GRAVE OF A WORLD!

I DISCOVERED MANY FASCINATING THINGS IN THAT DANK, ROTTING VILLAGE...

THESE VEGETABLES THEY RAISE FOR FOOD... THEY, TOO, HAVE BEEN AFFECTED BY THE STRANGE GAS THAT'S PART OF THE ATMOSPHERE... THEY, TOO, ARE MOVING BACK IN TIME!

YEARS AGO THOSE BEASTS MUST HAVE BEEN OXEN... BUT THE FETID AIR DOWN HERE HAS CHANGED THEM... AS IT HAS CHANGED EVERYTHING ELSE!

I SPENT MORE THAN A YEAR IN THAT TOMB OF A VILLAGE, AND THEN...

MY CHANCE FOR FREEDOM AT LAST! THOSE GUARDS... ASLEEP! IF I CAN GET PAST WITHOUT DISTURBING THEM...

FRESH AIR AT LAST! HOW CLEAN IT TASTES... HOW WONDERFUL TO BE BACK IN MY OWN WORLD AGAIN!

5

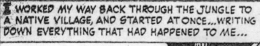

I WORKED MY WAY BACK THROUGH THE JUNGLE TO A NATIVE VILLAGE, AND STARTED AT ONCE...WRITING DOWN EVERYTHING THAT HAD HAPPENED TO ME...

IT...IT'S ONE OF THE GREATEST DISCOVERIES OF ALL TIMES! MY NAME WILL RANK AMONGST THE IMMORTALS OF SCIENCE!

I HAD BEEN WRITING FOR ABOUT THREE HOURS WHEN I NOTICED MY HAND...

THAT HAIR...THE POROUS, SLIMY FLESH...I...I'M CHANGING!

THAT GAS I BREATHED FOR A WHOLE YEAR...

IT...IT'S CHANGING ME!

I AM BECOMING...

ONE OF THEM!

I MUST GO BACK...BACK TO MY PEOPLE! HOW STRANGE THAT AT ONE TIME I THOUGHT THEM MONSTERS...

EEEYAHH!

...WHEN...IT...IT'S YOU...AND YOUR RACE WHO ARE MONSTERS! ONE DAY, I WILL COME TO THE SURFACE WITH MY PEOPLE...AND WE WILL RULE THE WORLD! HA! HA! HA!

THE END

WE DARE YOU TO READ THESE TALES OF TERROR and SUSPENSE
NOW PUBLISHED MONTHLY
THE BEST IN SHOCK MYSTERY
GET THEM EVERY MONTH
TALES OF TERROR AND SUSPENSE!
CHAMBER OF CHILLS
WE DARE YOU
WITCHES TALES
STRANGEST TALES of FEAR and SUPERSTITION!
BLACK CAT MYSTERY
TALES BEYOND BELIEF AND IMAGINATION
TOMB OF TERROR

Kiss of Horror!

He felt those wonderful arms surround his neck, he tasted the warm passion of her lips, and he knew that this was his life.

"Martha! Martha, I love you!"

"I know, darling, and perhaps I love you, too."

He swam in the ecstasy of the moment. She had to love him...she had to be his.

"Why are you so doubtful? Why can't you love me as I love you?"

"I never said I didn't, Tom. It's just that love must be more than love. You'll call me foolish again, but I must have power, wealth, security!"

"Then you will! And I'll give it to you!"

Her arms reached up to him and brought him down to waiting, eager lips.

Tom never forgot his promise. Martha would never let him. And the lips, the eyes, the form of Martha preyed on his heart and threw his mind toward evil!

Tom was but one of three partners in a small lumber business. The three worked hard together and a warm friendship had emerged. But the days that followed destroyed it all.

Tom lost his partners...and his friends... and profited by it. He leaped to the top of the business world by every evil means, and finally, Martha would have him.

They were married in a great and exquisite ceremony that was attended by every notable and every important newspaperman in the country. Everyone heard about it...everyone spoke about it.

After that, Tom raced still higher and higher in the world of finance—propelled by Martha. Lying and cheating became his daily diet, and still she hadn't enough...

Frisby came next. Poor Frisby whose company had the government contracts. Poor Frisby, whose single talent made his company the power it was!

"But, Martha..."

Those arms of hers reached out from the trap, and snared him...grasping him, bringing him to the passion of her lips...and the horror of her mind!

It wasn't long afterwards that William Frisby died a strange death, and days later that Tom gained the government contracts!

"What else can she drive me to? What other evil is there left for me to commit." Those were the thoughts he'd come home with each night. Those were the thoughts he came home with that night.

He was early. The amount of work had bludgeoned him, and he was starving for rest. His key silently turned the lock, and he wearily walked through the hallway. His eyes casually turned toward the living room and saw...

"Martha, Martha, I love you! I need you!"

"Peter, don't talk. Just kiss me...hold me tight to you...don't let me go!"

It was inevitable...it had to be this way... the circle had completed its route. But Peter, his own protege, the great mind of his business!

"GET OUT!" Tom's voice shook the room.

"T-T-Tom, I'm sorry...I'm ashamed..."

"It's not your fault, Peter. Just get out."

She was shameless...disgustingly nonchalant, as if he had come in on a chess game.

"Let me look at you, you wench! You she-beast! You horrible creature!"

"Hah, hah, hah, hah! You stupid fool, look at me! Look into my face and tell me what you see! Hah, hah!"

SLAPPP!

He slapped her, but her mad laughter went on!

"Look at me, fool, and tell me what you see!"

His eyes wiped away the rage. He gripped himself and looked...

"Aghhhhhhhhh!"

"Yes, you finally see me as I am! But only you can see it! Remember, for they won't believe you ...I am a witch! Hah, hah, hah!"

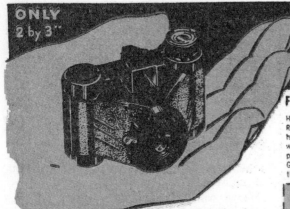

FRANK DARCY CRINGES IN SICKLY HORROR AS HE SEES THE SWIRLING EDDIES OF BLOOD...AS HIS EARS HUM WITH THE CEASELESS POUNDING OF THE MAMMOTH HEART FOR...IN THIS PULSATING BODY...HE HAS BECOME...

THE MAN GERM

NO! THEY...THEY'RE COMING TOWARDS ME...ARGHH!

A SAFARI STRETCHES OUT LIKE A SLITHERING EEL IN THE HOT, RANK JUNGLES OF AFRICA, AND...AT ITS HEAD IS FRANK DARCY...RELENTLESS...SWEATTY...

MOVE! I TOLD YOU TO MOVE.

MR. DARCY...THE MEN ARE SCARED. THEY GO SLOWLY. IT IS A SIGN...OF DOOM.

SHUT UP! I DON'T WANT ANY OF YOUR NATIVE IDIOCY.

THE SAFARI PLUNGED DEEPER INTO THE JUNGLE, PAST GREEN, GLOSSY FOLIAGE, STRANGE BIRDS JABBERED OMINOUSLY OVERHEAD...UNTIL...

GOT TO...A CITY. *A LOST CITY.* GREAT SCOTT! WHAT IS THAT?

WHY...IT'S BIGGER THAN A COLOSSUS. I'M GOING TO...

NO, DO NOT GO NEAR IT!

WHAT?!! COME BACK YOU FOOLS!

THEY WILL NOT RETURN. THEY THINK IT'S *ALIVE*...AND THAT YOU WILL HARM IT!

I'M GOING TO FIND OUT WHAT'S *INSIDE* THAT THING. I DIDN'T COME ALL THIS WAY...FOR NOTHING

I DO NOT WANT TO STAY, MR. DARCY. I LEAVE. THERE IS DEATH IN THAT STATUE. I *WARN* YOU!

ALONE...ON THE FOOT OF A MUTE GOLIATH THAT TOWERED OVER HIM...DARCY SEEMED MICROSCOPIC...A BACILLUS WHOSE MINUTE STING WAS A PICK-AXE.

WHEW! CAN'T SEEM TO DENT IT. DON'T UNDERSTAND IT. SOFT, TOO! ALMOST LIKE...SKIN.

SOON...

THERE! A HOLE BIG ENOUGH TO LET ME THROUGH.

DARCY LOWERED HIMSELF DEEPER INTO THE CAVITY HE TORE FROM THE STATUE'S FOOT. DEEPER...INTO SLIMY DREGS THAT ELICITED AN ACRID, FETID ODOR...STRONG...

WHAT A SMELL. I WONDER... WHAT...THE *HOLE IS CLOSING.*

SUDDENLY...

UGH-H-H! I'M *STUCK!* I--I'M BEING *SUCKED UNDER!*

WHERE...*WHERE AM I?* GOOD LORD! I'M SWIMMING IN...*BLOOD.* IT'S...*BLOOD.* I-I CAN'T...

THE BLOOD RUSHED TOWARDS DARCY. IT SURGED, ENGULFING HIM IN DEATH-LIKE CONVULSIONS. TWISTING, CRIMSON WHIRLPOOLS THAT BROUGHT...

EEEYAHH! SOMETHING'S GOT MY FOOT. *GLURRGH!*

SHAPELESS CELLS...THAT HAD TO BE FED.

ARGHH! THOSE TENTACLES! STABBING FOR ME! IT...IT...*WAIT!* THIS SHELL IS THIN. IF I...IF I CAN *BREAK THRU IT* ...GOT TO. UNHH!

DARCY'S BODY BECAME A SEETHING CAULDRON OF STRENGTH. UNHOLY, EERIE DEATH LOOMED SUDDENLY. THE CELL'S WALL GAVE... AND DARCY SCRAMBLED THROUGH THE HOLE, RISING SWIFTLY...SILENTLY...UPWARD IN THE SEA OF BLOOD.

TIRED...BUT...GOT TO GO ON. NOW...THAT I KNOW... *WHAT I AM.* THAT CELL *COLLAPSED* BECAUSE...

SUDDENLY...

I'M A GERM. THE STATUE *IS ALIVE.* I....*AIEEEE!* CORPUSCLES! THE STATUE'S *CORPUSCLES!*

RUN! RUN! THEY'LL *EAT ME* IF I'M CAUGHT. *RUUNNN!*

DARCY RACED WILDLY THROUGH THE CAVERNOUS DEPTHS OF THE STATUE'S LIVING BODY. STILL THE GAPING CORPUSCLES CAME AFTER HIM...A FOREIGN ELEMENT THAT HAD TO BE DEVOURED. DARCY CLIMBED...TOWARDS...

THE PORES. I'LL TRY TO *PUSH THROUGH* THE PORES.

I CAN'T! I...I'M *TRAPPED!* NO-O-O!

RAVENOUS GROWLS OF HUNGER ROSE WITHIN THE MONSTERS AS THEY CREPT TO DARCY. THEN...AS HE SPRAWLED OVER A CLAMMY, DANK TISSUE...HE SAW...

WHAT IS *THAT?* I'VE *GOT TO USE IT*...WHATEVER IT IS!

THIS MUST BE AN *ARTERY!* BUT, WHICH ONE? *WHERE DOES IT LEAD?*

THEN DARCY HEARD IT: THE ECHOING RUMBLE...THE MUFFLED, RHYTHMIC POUNDING...

OHHH. MY EARS! THAT *OBJECT* AHEAD...DRAWING ME TO IT...SOUNDS LIKE A *PULSE BEAT.*

IT'S... *THE HEART.* I'M BEING *FED RIGHT INTO IT.*

FRANK DARCY TOPPLED FROM THE PRECIPICE OF LIFE. MERCILESSLY, HE WAS CRUSHED BY THE STATUE'S THROBBING HEART. BUT...

...HIS POSITION OF DEATH IMPEDED THE HEART'S MOVEMENT. SOON, IT STOPPED...AND THE GHASTLY SILENCE INDICATED THE STATUE'S CESSATION OF LIFE. IT FELL. THUS, FRANK DARCY ...LIKE ALL GERMS... CARRIED THE VENOM OF EVIL.

THE END

Stories behind the STARS

HYDRA THE IMMORTAL MONSTER

HYDRA, THE MONSTROUS SERPENT WAS RAVAGING THE COUNTRY OF ARGOS. ITS HORRIBLE HEADS SPIT STREAMS OF FLAMES THAT EVEN MELTED STONE!

IN ORDER TO STOP THIS BLOODY MASSACRE, THE GODS SENT HERCULES TO FIGHT AND KILL HYDRA. BEFORE THE TERRIBLE BATTLE HERCULES CALLED FOR STRENGTH...

THEN, THE STRUGGLE BEGAN! BUT AS HERCULES CHOPPED OFF ONE OF THE MONSTER'S HEADS, TWO NEW HEADS GREW IN ITS PLACE. FINALLY, ANOTHER WARRIOR IOLAUS, WAS SENT TO HELP HERCULES. AS HERCULES CHOPPED OFF A HEAD, IOLAUS WOULD SEAL THE STUMP WITH A HOT IRON, AND SO THE HEADS COULD NOT GROW BACK.

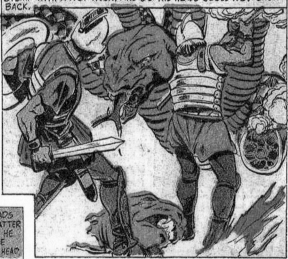

ONE OF THE GODS, JUNO DISLIKED HERCULES AND SENT A GIANT CRAB TO BITE HIM ON THE FOOT, HOWEVER, HERCULES TOOK CARE OF THE CRAB...

ONE OF THE MONSTER'S HEADS WAS IMMORTAL, AND NO MATTER HOW HARD HERCULES TRIED HE COULD NOT KILL THE SNAKE BECAUSE OF THIS IMMORTAL HEAD.

THE TWO WARRIORS MADE A DARING MOVE, THEY RETREATED TO A NEARBY HILL AS HYDRA FOLLOWED THEM. THEN, THEY HURLED DOWN HUGE BOULDERS AND COMPLETELY BURIED THE MONSTER...

HYDRA NEVER APPEARED ON EARTH AGAIN, BUT TO THIS VERY DAY YOU CAN SEE IT HIGH UP IN THE HEAVENS.

REGULUS

PROCYON

HYDRA

ALPHARD

SO THEY'RE SAVAGES, ARE THEY? ARE THEY! ROCCO MASTY THOUGHT THEY WERE. HE LAUGHED AT THEIR LAWS...DEFILED THEM GREEDILY AND LUSTFULLY! BUT, VERY SOON AFTER, HE HAD TO FACE...

THE THINGS!

IN A DIRTY CAFE ON THE GOLD COAST, A TIRED CANDLE GASHES OUT DEEP SCOWLS OF THOUGHT ON THE FACES OF THREE MEN...

THAT'S RIGHT, ALDO, NO ONE EVER GUARDS THE IDOL...

...EXCEPT A CURSE...

...AND THAT AIN'T GONNA STOP US FROM GETTIN' MILLIONS IN GEMS OUTA THE HEAD OF THE IDOL!

OKAY, THEN! WE START FOR WALLA LAND, TOMORROW.

YOU KNOW, THIS IS ONE TRIP WHICH IS SURE NECESSARY!

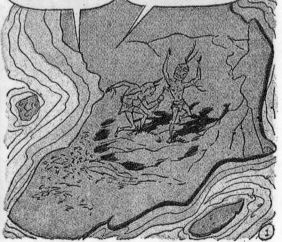

THE NEXT DAY... WE BEEN GOING FOR SIX HOURS NOW. BY NIGHT WE SHOULD REACH THE IDOL.

WALKIN' THROUGH THIS JUNGLE IS LIKE CRAWLIN' ACROSS A *SPIDER WEB!*

AS NIGHT SPREAD ITS BLANKET OF MYSTERY AND RESTLESSNESS OVER THE THROBBING JUNGLE...

ROCCO... MEZZI... *LOOK!*

LOOK AT IT SHINE!

AWRIGHT, STOP GAPING, YOU APES! WE GOT WORK TO DO!

FEVERISH, LUSTFUL MINUTES PASS!

WHAT A BUNCH OF DOPES, THEM WALLAS...THINKING A CURSE WOULD GUARD THE IDOL!

IT'S A WONDER NOBODY ELSE DIDN'T GET OUR IDEA AND COME HERE BEFORE.

AH, THEY SAY SOME GUYS TRIED BUT WERE FOUND DEAD LATER. THEY SAID THEIR BODIES WERE EATEN AWAY!

THEY PROBABLY GOT THE JUNGLE FEVER! NOW SHUT UP ABOUT THE CURSE AND LET'S GET OUT OF HERE!

Y-YEAH, SURE, ROCCO!

UNKNOWN TO THE THREE TRESPASSERS OF THE GODS, A RED FLUID OOZES FROM THE GOUGED WOUNDS IN THE HEAD OF THE IDOL. ACCORDING TO LEGEND, THIS MARKS THE BEGINNING OF THE CURSE!

AIEEHHH! AGAIN THE IDOL OF WALLAH HAS BEEN DEFILED. DEATH TO THE SINNERS...*DEATH!*

LATER... FEAST YOUR EYES ON THAT, MY BOYS! THERE'S ENOUGH MONEY THERE TO RUN THE WORLD!

ONE HANDFUL AND WE'D BE RICHER THAN ALL THE KINGS OF EUROPE!

AN' I WAS AFRAID OF A CURSE!

2

EYES BULGE WITH HORROR WHICH WAS BEFORE SUPPRESSED ...BUT WHICH WAS NOW UNLEASHED IN A WILD FURY!

WHAT'S THAT SOUND?

I HEARD SOMETHING LIKE THAT ONCE! ARMY ANTS!

ARMY ANTS! LET'S GET OUTSIDE... *QUICK!*

TUMBLING OUTSIDE AND RUNNING SEVERAL HUNDRED YARDS DOWN THE ROAD, THE THREE MEN SAW...

...THE *BLACK ANTS!*

NOOO! THEY CAN EAT THROUGH STONE!

THAT'S WHY THEY FOUND THE OTHERS WITH THE FLESH EATEN OFF THEIR BONES!

SSSSSSS

A MILLION CRUNCHING, TEARING JAWS SLICE AHEAD... AHEAD... AHEAD...

C'MON BACK TO THE SHACK! THEY'RE STILL FAR AWAY. IT'LL TAKE THEM A WHILE TO REACH US!

THEY'RE ALL AROUND US! THEY'VE GOT US SURROUNDED!

WHAT ARE WE GOIN' TO DO? WHAT ARE WE GOIN' TO DO?

HERES WHAT WE'LL DO. WE'LL DIG A MOAT AROUND THE SHACK! THEN WE'LL POUR THAT GASOLINE WE HIJACKED INTO IT AND SET IT ON FIRE. C'MON!

YEAH... THAT'S IT! THATS IT!

THE PERSPIRATION OF FEAR AND FATIGUE POPPED OUT AS HUGE GLOBULES ON THE FOREHEADS OF THE MEN...

JUST A LITTLE MORE!

THEY'RE ALMOST ON TOP OF US!

SSSSSS

THEN, THE GASOLINE WAS POURED INTO THE RAVAGED PIT AND THE BATTLE WAS ABOUT TO BEGIN!

HERE THEY COME! GIMME THE TORCH!

IT'S GOTTA STOP THEM! IT'S GOTTA.'

HERE, ROCCO!

3

AS THE ANTS REACH THE MOAT, A FLAMING TORCH SPLASHES INTO THE GASOLINE AND SHOOTS UP A WALL OF *FIRE!*

AND SO THE HORROR CONTINUED. OVER AND OVER AGAIN, THE ANTS TRIED TO CROSS THE SEA OF FIRE. BUT, THEN...

WHAT! THEY'RE PUSHING ROCKS TO THE MOAT!

THEY'RE GONNA FILL UP THE MOAT AND THEN CROSS OVER AND GET US!

THOSE THINGS'LL GET US, BUT MAYBE NOT! MAYBE ALL THEY WANT IS A COUPLE OF VICTIMS TO SATISFY THE CURSE!

DESPERATION FIRES THE BRAIN OF ROCCO WITH A MAD PLAN...

SORRY, GUYS, BUT IT'S EITHER YOU OR ME!

NO, ROCCO, NO...ARRGGH!

UGHHH...

BAM BAM BANG!

NOW TO APPEASE THOSE MONSTERS OUT THERE. I'LL THROW THEM THE BODIES. MAYBE THEN THEY'LL LEAVE...

ALDO'S CORPSE PLUNGES CRAZILY THROUGH THE AIR AND SINKS DEEPLY INTO THE RANKS OF THE ANT. THE SAME THAT HAPPENS TO HIM...

...HAPPENS TO MEZZI'S CORPSE!

BUT THE TWO SACRIFICES DO NOT SATISFY THE APPETITE OF THE MADDENED ANTS. IN FACT...

THEY...THEY'RE CARRYING ALDO'S AND MEZZI'S BONES TO THE EDGE OF THE MOAT. THEY'RE GOING TO USE THE BONES AS A BRIDGE TO GET ME!

HAVING ALREADY ESTABLISHED A FOUNDATION OF ROCKS, THE ANTS NEED BUT THE BONES TO COMPLETE THEIR SPANNING THE MOAT. THROUGH ROCCO'S MIND DARTS THE REMEMBRANCE OF THE CURSE...

THEY'RE USING THE BONES OF THE MEN I MURDERED TO MURDER ME. HA...HAAA!

AND THEN THE THINGS CAME, SNAPPING, SAVAGE, SEEKING...

AIEEEHH!!

...SEEKING THE LAST OF THOSE WHO HAD DARED CHALLENGE THE CURSE OF WALLA!

THE END.

5

CLUTCHING FINGERS

The moon skimmed the surface of the water, tipping the shadowed waves with pale, glinting silver. The sea was unnaturally calm ... a vast pool of solitude ... an inky span of nothingness. The air was heavy with a nameless dread ... a thick, choking waitingness ...

"Peter!" The girl's voice wafted lightly from the shore, carried away on the streams of stillness. "I—I've changed my mind! L—let's not go swimming! There's something about the water ... something weird ... it—it *frightens* me!"

"Don't be silly! It's just that the night's so hot and sticky! Come on, honey! Last one in is a coward!"

Peter Bane splashed gaily into the surf, his smoothly-tanned body gleaming white in the moonlight. The water was unexpectedly warm, and Peter dove headfirst into the breakers, seeking relief from the thick humidity of the air. Down ... down ... down ...

"Peter!" Marjorie Bane's voice was shrill with terror. "Peter! Where are you?!" Her breath rattled in her throat as she dove in after her husband. Clutching fingers, slimy, slippery, slithering fingers wound themselves around her arms, her legs, dragging her down ... down ... down to the very bowels of the earth beneath the sea ...

She opened her eyes to find herself in Peter's arms. It was hot, hot with a dry, burning heat, wherever they were. The sibilant hiss of rushing water was loud in their ears, but no water was to be seen. They seemed to be trapped in a smooth-walled, airless cell of some kind ... fathoms deep.

"I—I guess you were right, honey!" Peter murmured with a feeble attempt at humor. "We shouldn't have gone swimming tonight ... !"

The heavy steel door of the cell clanged open. For an instant there was only emptiness, and then ... dark, wet shapes swarmed through the door, filling the tiny room with their foul breath, the acrid stench of their bodies. Their clammy, octopus-like tentacles lashed out, stinging, ripping, hungry for blood ... human blood ...

The Banes battled desperately, wordlessly, their terror too naked, too stark even for screams. With their bare hands they ripped the gashing tentacles from their bodies, struck out blindly against the jelly-like monsters that slithered around them. The sickening squash of splattered jelly echoed dully from wall to wall.

The tearing sound of ripped open flesh slashed through the gloom as the merciless razor-like tentacles struck again ... and again ... and again. The drip of human blood kept time with the hideous, suckling sounds of a thousand monster-mouths eagerly lapping up every spilled drop ...

Consciousness ebbed away, and Peter and Marjorie Bane surrendered gratefully to the darkness ... the velvet, comforting darkness of death. And then—suddenly—the darkness lifted. The warm, slow-moving waves of the sea bathed their bruised and battered bodies, revived their numb and horror-clouded brains.

Somehow—some way—they were free! The cell was gone ... the blood-sucking jellyfish were gone ... the night air was cool and heavy on their faces ...

"Don't try to talk, dearest!" Peter cautioned as they dragged themselves up to the beach. "Not yet ... "

"Kraaaaaghh!!" Marjorie Bane's voice, hoarse and wild, croaked a chilling chant of death. She seized her husband's wrist, dragging him back into the sea—the calm, waiting, silver-tipped sea. Gray, sticky jelly oozed from the gashes on her hand, and where the fingers should have been there were only clammy, clutching tentacles ...

CHAMBER OF CHILLS

TALES OF TERROR AND SUSPENSE!

CHAMBER OF CHILLS

magazine

10¢

NO. 14
NOV

...OND BELIEF!
...RROR SPAWNED
...THE BOWELS
...THE EARTH!
...VE UP ALL HOPE
...YOU STEP...
...EP... STEP...
...OWN
...O
...EATH!

Lee Elias

CHAMBER OF CHILLS MAGAZINE, NOVEMBER, 1952, Vol. 1, No. 14, IS PUBLISHED MONTHLY by WITCHES TALES, INC., 1860 Broadway, New York 23, N.Y. Entered as second class matter at the Post Office at New York, N.Y. under the Act of March 3, 1879. Single copies 10c. Subscription rates. 10 issues for $1.00 in the U.S. and possessions, elsewhere $1.50. All names in this periodical are entirely fictitious and no identification with actual persons is intended. Contents copyrighted, 1952, by Witches Tales, Inc., New York City. Printed in the U.S.A.

The time of terror has arrived once more . . . the crash of the door has sealed all exits . . . tension mounts to a suspenseful crescendo . . . and you are caught in the CHAMBER OF CHILLS!

No escape . . . no way out! You have come to the lair of Satan! You have arrived at the most fitful scenes imaginable! You are trapped within the loathsome corridors . . . snared in the never ending labyrinths of the CHAMBER OF CHILLS!

Come one—come all, if you dare—and see the horror spectacles of the ages. Read the most thrilling tales ever lived . . . be gripped by the tentacles of terror!

Wonder at . . . hide from . . . fight . . . flee from . . . IT! Cast your eyes on IT's most horrendous secret and know that you have found infinite horror!

Watch your steps as they carry you ever on . . . ever downward! Beware the magnet that draws its prey DOWN TO DEATH!

At every corner. . . . in every door . . . behind the mouldings of the walls lurks the incredible creature they call the SPIDER MAN!

And learn the evil mysteries that live in a piece of jewelry . . . jewelry that has been branded now and forever as the DEVIL'S NECKLACE!

All this and more awaits you in the masterpiece of mystery and terror, the saga of the supernatural that we have called the . . .

CHAMBER OF CHILLS!

CHAMBER OF CHILLS

CONTENTS NOV. No. 14

THE COLD, GRIMY BLOCKS OF GRANITE...THE PULPY SLOP OF CEMENT RANCID WITH THE STENCH OF DEATH...THE PIERCING SCRAPE OF THE SEPULCHRAL TROWEL...ALL THIS AS THE SINISTER MASONS BUILD...

THEY'VE COME AGAIN! DOING THEIR WORK...ALWAYS WORKING! BUT... WHAT ARE THEY BUILDING?

THREE MEN STOOD BEFORE A GRAVEYARD, THE TOMBSTONES DECAYED... GNAWED ROTTEN BY THE TEETH OF TIME...

I WANT YOU TO BUILD MY MANSION

BUT, MR. DRESDEN... THAT'S A...A CEME-TARY! IT'S BEEN THERE FOR AGES!

I DON'T CARE! DIG IT UP! AND START BUILDING!

RIGHT AWAY, MR. DRESDEN!

THAT NIGHT, DRESDEN FELT THE FINGERS OF SLEEP APPROACH... BUT THEY CAME GNARLED AND TWISTED, ENCLOSING HIM IN A WORLD OF BLACK, HIDEOUS NIGHT-MARES!

TOOLS-- GRANITE WHY WHY CLANK CLANK

WHAT IS THAT?

CLANK! CLANK! CLANK!

WHAT TH'... THOSE MEN... THEY'RE BUILDING WITH THOSE TOOLS...

THEY'RE WORKING ON MY PROPERTY! I'LL PUT A STOP TO THAT!

BUT DRESDEN FOUND... ONLY THE HAUNTING SILENCE... AND A LOW WALL, PUZZLING AND SINISTER IN ITS UNFINISHED BEGINNINGS...

THEY'VE GONE! BUILT THIS WALL, EH? I'LL SHOW THEM THEY CAN'T BUILD HERE!

BUUUNNNGG!!

I'LL... I'LL DEMOLISH IT! UNNN-H! WHY...THE HAMMER BOUNCES RIGHT OFF! IT'S HARDLY DENTED! I DON'T UNDERSTAND!

3

THE NEXT NIGHT, KARL DRESDEN WAITED IN THE WISPED SHADOWS, THROBBING WITH CURIOSITY... AND FEAR!

THAT UNFINISHED WALL... SOMETHING EERIE ABOUT IT! I'VE GOT TO KNOW WHAT IT IS!

I THOUGHT I SAW SOMETHING! YES! THERE THEY ARE! LORD... HOW UGLY... ALMOST HUMAN!

...AND...THEY'RE BUILDING AGAIN!

THE HOURS TICKED BY... THE WALL GROWING LIKE A MONSTER... ITS NERVES THE SLIMY, DRIPPING CEMENT SEEMS! SUDDENLY...

HOW LONG?...WAIT, THEY'RE GOING! NOW I'LL FIND OUT WHAT THEY'RE BUILDING!

IT...IT LOOKS LIKE A HUT! NO...IT COULDN'T BE THAT! I CAN'T SEEM TO MAKE IT OUT!

WHAT IS IT! WHY IS IT HERE? WHY?!!

4

STRANGE SUPERSTITIONS

IN VENICE OF THE FOURTEENTH CENTURY, THE OPAL WAS ASSOCIATED WITH THE BLACK DEATH! THE SUPERSTITION WAS THAT THE OPAL MARKED ITS OWNER'S DEATH FROM THE PLAGUE BY EMITTING HUES FOR SEVERAL SECONDS!

SOME PRIMITIVE PEOPLE BELIEVED THAT THE MOON WAS THE 'ABODE OF THE DEAD!' THE PALE FACE OF THE MOON CONVINCED THEM THAT THIS WAS SO!

A SUPERSTITION IN THE DEEP SOUTH IS THAT THE PRAYING MANTIS IS AN AGENT OF THE DEVIL AND, IF DISTURBED, WILL TURN UPON ITS VICTIM AND STRIKE HIM BLIND!

IN SPAIN IT IS BELIEVED BY MANY THAT THE HARE VENTURES INTO GRAVEYARDS AT NIGHT AND DIGS UP DEAD BODIES! FOR THIS REASON, THE HARE IS NEVER EATEN IN THAT COUNTRY!

DURING THE MIDDLE AGES, IT WAS THOUGHT THAT ON ALL HALLOWS EVE, SATAN WOULD TAKE THE FORM OF A HIDEOUS BLACK CAT WHILE CONSORTING WITH THE WITCHES THROUGHOUT THE NIGHT!

TO THE AMERICAN INDIANS, THE OWL IS THE SPIRIT OF A DEAD SOUL, TAKING THAT FORM TO GIVE WARNING OF APPROACHING DEATH! THEY BELIEVED THAT THE BIRD WAS THE PULSE OR HEARTBEAT OF THE DEAD PERSON WHO CAME TO TELL NEWS IN THE GLOOM OF MIDNIGHT!

AND EONS PASSED BY, HERALDING THE COMING OF NEW THINGS, NEW FORMS OF LIFE--WHILE THE GIANT REPTILES AND DINOSAURS RULED THE EARTH...

EEEEEEEEAAARGHHH!

THE WATERS DRIED UP--NEW OCEANS ROSE AND FELL--THE EARTH CRACKED OPEN AND CLOSED AGAIN--AND NOW IN LABYRINTHS OF STEAMING MUD, WAS CRADLED THE INVADER FROM THE SKIES--AND A NEWLY FORMED EMBRYO...

TIME SPED BY--AND THE EMBRYO FORMED INTO A SICKLY-LOOKING, STRINGY CREATURE WHICH DEVELOPED AND MATURED INTO A FURRED MONSTROSITY! THE ALIEN WAS AWAKENED AT LAST--ALIVE AND HUNGRY!

FOOD! I MUST HAVE FOOD! I HUNGER FOR LIFE-FORCE!

WAIT--I SENSE THE MIND-EMANATIONS OF STRANGE SURFACE-BEINGS! YES--THEY ARE THE FOOD I SEEK! BUT I MUST DEVISE A PLAN FOR CONSTANT SUPPLY! I MUST STUDY THEM WELL...

THOUSANDS OF YEARS WENT BY AGAIN, AND NOW, THE ALIEN HORROR WAS READY. PETER TRASK WAS ON HIS LAST STAGES OF COMPLETE COLLAPSE, AS A MAN, HE WAS A DUD! AS A PROSPECTOR--HE WAS EVEN A WORSE FAILURE...

I GOTTA FIND GOLD... IT'S MY ONLY CHANCE TO GO INTO TOWN AGAIN... GOLD... .

HELLO! WHAT'S THIS? WELL, I'LL BE--THIS CAVE LEADS INTO SOME SORT O' CHAMBER...MAYBE THERE'S GOLD INSIDE!

2

TRASK WALKED FURTHER INTO THE GLOOM..AS THE ROTTING, FETID SLIME OF PREHISTORIC FOSSILS GURGLED INCESSANTLY IN THE OOZE...

GOOD GOD! I--I'D NEVER O' BELIEVED IT IF I HADN'T SEEN IT WITH MY OWN EYES!

LOOK! THERE'S AN OPEN CHAMBER OVER THERE! WHY--THIS HERE CAVE IS A HONEYCOMB OF GROTTOS! WHO WOULD O' EVER THOUGHT IT?

THERE MUST BE GOLD HERE! I'M SURE! W-WHAT'S THAT? Y---AHH!

A-A-A-A-G-H-H-HH!

DO NOT BE ALARMED, PETER TRASK! I SHALL NOT HARM YOU-- IF YOU DO AS I SAY! I AM AILOS, ALIEN TO YOUR PLANET. IT IS YOU I HAVE SELECTED TO BE MY LURE!

D-DON'T K-KILL ME... P-PLEASE! I--I'LL DO ANYTHING Y-YOU SAY -- PLEASE!

I DESIRE HUMAN FOOD...HUMANS THAT ARE ALIVE! AND YOU SHALL DELIVER ONE TO ME EVERY TWENTY-FOUR HOURS. IN RETURN YOU WILL HAVE ANYTHING AND EVERYTHING -- FOR MY EXTRAORDINARY MIND CAN INFLUENCE THE WILL OF MEN!

Y-YES...YES!

3

THUS, WAS THE UNHOLY BOND CEMENTED WITH TERROR AND GREED! PETER TRASK KEPT HIS BARGAIN. HE WENT TO HIS HATED ENEMY, WALTER LEECH, AND PROMISED HIM MUCH GOLD. AND LEECH FELL INTO THE TRAP...

--IT'S IN HERE, YOU SAY? TRASK--IF YOU TRY ANYTHING FUNNY, I'LL---

NO-! NO! YOU'LL SEE! JUST A FEW FEET MORE--!

I DON'T LIKE IT! I BETTER--- AAAIIEEE!

HA, HA...FOOD! FOOD!

AH! WARM BLOOD! YOU HAVE DONE WELL, MY FRIEND! GO NOW--AND REMEMBER TO BE BACK TOMORROW WITH MORE!

UGHHH... Y-YES...

THAT VERY DAY, OIL WAS FOUND ON PETER TRASK'S DILAPIDATED FARM. AND TWO MONTHS LATER, THE EX-BEGGAR WAS AN OIL MILLIONAIRE.

HERE'S A CHECK FOR $500,000! I THINK IT WILL SUFFICIENTLY COVER YOUR FIRST PROFIT!

I WANT IT IN DOLLAR BILLS--SO I CAN COUNT IT FOR MYSELF!

AND ALWAYS, ANOTHER VICTIM WAS LED TO THAT GROTTO BENEATH THE EARTH! SUSPICION WAS DIVERTED AWAY FROM TRASK THROUGH THE MIND-FORCE OF THE TERRIBLE CREATURE THAT LURKED BELOW--AND THE HUMAN TRAITOR BECAME A MULTI-MILLIONAIRE...

HERE'S SOME MORE COINS! HA, HA...

IT'S MINE!

NO! I SAW IT FIRST!

TRASK OVERCAME HIS INITIAL DISGUST OF HIS MASTER'S HABITS. TO HIM, IT WAS PART OF A NECESSARY BUSINESS...

DID I NOT PROMISE YOU SOFT FLESH THIS TIME, AILOS?

YES! SLURP...SLURP...YOU ARE AN EXCELLENT LURE! YOU SHALL HAVE YOUR FORTUNE OF PRECIOUS GEMS!

4

PETER TRASK BECAME A POWER TO BE RECKONED WITH. ALL WEALTH AND INFLUENCE LED TO HIM. POLITICIANS, FINANCIERS, CAPTAINS OF INDUSTRY BECAME HIS CHATTEL...

PLEASE, MR. TRASK! YOU MUST LEND ME THE REQUIRED SUM! I'LL BE RUINED!

I'M SORRY, DENTON! LEAVE AT ONCE--OR I'LL HAVE YOU ARRESTED!

NOW RICH, POWERFUL, FAMOUS, TRASK NEEDED ONLY A WIFE TO MAKE HIM HAPPY. HE GOT HIS WISH...

--I NOW PRONOUNCE YOU MAN AND WIFE! YOU MAY KISS THE BRIDE!

WITH PLEASURE!

BUT ONE NIGHT HE FOUND SOMETHING HE HADN'T RECKONED WITH...

HOW LONG CAN WE GO ON LIKE THIS, MYRA!? WE MUST TELL HIM!

NO, HARRY! YOU DON'T KNOW HIM! HE'LL KILL US BOTH!

WE MUSTN'T EVER BE SEEN HERE TOGETHER AGAIN! BUT WE CAN MEET IN A SMALL RENDEZVOUS I'VE SET UP IN THE DESERT! HE'LL NEVER KNOW!

I'LL CHOKE THEM BOTH WITH MY BARE HANDS! NO---! I HAVE A BETTER IDEA...

PETER TRASK BIDED HIS TIME UNTIL HARRY LEFT. THEN, ONCE ON THE HIGHWAY, HE PUT HIS DIABOLICAL PLAN INTO OPERATION...

HE'S ALMOST NEARING THE GROTTO OF AILOS! GOOD! HE'LL NEVER GO ANYPLACE AGAIN! HA, HA...

BAAROOOM!

SCREEEECH!

5

BAH! *AILOS* WON'T WANT DEAD BODIES! IT'S JUST AS WELL, HOWEVER! NO ONE SAW ME KILL HIM! WAIT! THERE'S SOMEONE OUT THERE! SOMEONE'S FOLLOWED ME!

*S*MOOTHLY, GRACEFULLY, TRASK AROSE AND WALKED SLOWLY INSIDE THE GROTTO, MAKING SURE HIS UNKNOWN FOLLOWER WAS BEHIND HIM. THEN, WHEN HE HAD REACHED THE BRINK OF THE MONSTER'S DEN....

DOWN YOU GO, SUCKER! HA, HA...THAT'S THE END OF YOU!

SMAACKK!

THE FALL ISN'T HIGH ENOUGH TO KILL ANYONE--ONLY STUN HIM! GOOD! AILOS HAS MY VICTIM FOR TODAY! HA, HA...

AILOS! I'VE BROUGHT YOU ANOTHER--OHHH ---IT'S MYRA! *SHE'S* THE ONE THAT FOLLOWED ME! BUT WHY DOESN'T SHE COME TO? *WHY?*

SHE IS DEAD, FOOL! A FRAGILE WOMAN IS NO MATCH FOR A FALL SUCH AS THIS! YOU HAVE KILLED MY ONLY OTHER *LURE!*

Y-YOU MEAN-- THAT S-SHE WAS--? N-NO ---*DON'T!* YA-A-AAH!

YES! SHE WAS BRINGING HER IMPETUOUS FRIEND TO ME! BUT NOW-- SHE IS DEAD-- AND SINCE YOU HAVE *NOT* BROUGHT A *LIVE* VICTIM YOURSELF-- I CANNOT ENDURE!

AH--IT IS GOOD TO EAT! AND I AM TRULY FOND OF SUCH TENDER MEAT! PERHAPS I CAN OFFER SOME SMALL GIFT AS AN EXPRESSION OF MY GRATITUDE? YOU OUT THERE HAVE LEARNED OF MY EXISTENCE! WOULD *YOU* CARE TO BE MY--- REPRESENTATIVE?

THE END

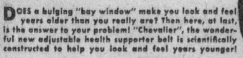

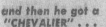

FLIGHT INTO THE PAST

Is it possible to take a flight into the past?

It not only is, but such flights have been recorded in the unexplained history of the world.

For instance, toward the end of World War II, an American officer in France was on leave. He found an interesting old art shop in a French city and spent his time browsing around. A Frenchman came up to him and asked him if he would be interested in original drawings. The officer said he was, and the Frenchman invited him to his chateau nearby.

There the Frenchman showed the officer exquisite drawings, prints and etchings, by the great masters.

Some time later the officer returned to the town and his first thought was to pay respects to the Frenchman. He reached the chateau only to find it a desolate ruin. From the natives, the officer learned that nobody had lived in the castle for 75 years, and that the last owner was a wealthy man who collected art masterpieces.

This is not an only instance.

In England, a few miles from the city of Bath, there lies the only ancient Anglo-Saxon church still in existence. Experts believe it was built during the tenth century.

One Sunday in 1932, Mrs. Eileen J. Garrett visited the church. As she examined it with her friends, Mr. and Mrs. Barber, she was struck by one fact. The navel and the choir section seemed to have changed in a matter of minutes!

She heard sounds of music and loud voices chanting in prayer. She found a spyhole and looked out into the courtyard.

At that time, the little church had been surrounded by modern buildings. But instead of buildings, Mrs. Garrett saw a large courtyard filled with people. They were dressed in costumes of the fifteenth century! And each of them seemed miserable!

Mrs. Garrett turned around. Instead of hoary church ruins, she saw she was in a well-kept church and priests and monks were passing by, one looking at her. And suddenly she felt something push her and suddenly she fell and knocked her head against a stone.

When she recovered consciousness, she was back in the twentieth century. She had a nasty bump on the back of her head, where she had been struck by a stone that had disappeared centuries ago!

She found that during the fourteenth and fifteenth centuries, there were leper colonies near the old church. They were not allowed inside the churches and said their mass outside in the courtyard!

Sometimes an incident happens in a given time and at a given hour. Afterwards it repeats itself at the given hour, regardless of time.

One such timeless place is an old house on St. Charles Avenue in New Orleans, La. The Devil is said to have lived there and he had taken a French wife. The Devil was fond of her and quite jealous, but at times he had to leave her to attend to other duties. During his absence, the French woman fell in love with a dashing young Creole man.

The Devil returned and waited for the Creole. He took him aside and told him that he knew . . . and would consent to his marrying the French woman provided that they must always be known as Mr. and Mrs. L.

The Creole told the French woman, who was terrified, for she knew "L" stood for Lucifer. In her rage, she took a towel and strangled the Creole. Upon this, the Devil came into her room and killed her. Then he took the two bodies to the roof and in full moonlight, he ate them except for the skins, which he fed to cats.

The Devil had made a mistake. He had eaten under the full moon, something forbidden to him. For this reason, he had to return again and again, and the whole scene of the meeting with the rival, the murders and the aftermath had to be repeated! People who rented the house left sickened after having been transported into the past and forced to witness all of it.

THE NEXT DAY...

I TELL YOU, GENTLEMEN! I HAVE SUCCEEDED! MY SECRET FLUID WILL WORK ON MANKIND!

THAT'S THE MOST PREPOSTEROUS THING I EVER HEARD!

IDIOTS! THEY DON'T REALIZE THE GENIUS OF CHARLES FRAGE!

CONFERENCE ROOM

SLAM

LATER THAT NIGHT A STRANGE EXPERIMENT TAKES PLACE!

REBUKE ME, WILL THEY! THEY'LL SOON LEARN OF THE POWER OF MY SPIDER FLUID! THIS SICKLY ANIMAL SHALL RESPOND TO THE SERUM!

AND AS THE PROFESSOR SLEEPS, THE DOG RESPONDS TO THE SPIDER FLUID! BUT IN A MANNER TOO HORRIBLE TO CONTEMPLATE!

AGGGEOW

AGGGGG!

WARPED BY THE IMPERFECT SERUM, THE HIDEOUS SPIDER-LIKE CREATURE THAT ONCE WAS A DOG, RACES OUT INTO THE NIGHT!

AGGGGGGEOW

2

AND OUTSIDE A DORMITORY...

AGGGREOW

IT'S HORRIBLE! AIEEEE!

AIEEEE! HELP-P!

BUT THE GIRL'S STARTLED SHRIEK SUMMONS HER CLASSMATES!

IT'S FANTASTIC!

HALF DOG, HALF SPIDER!

BLAM!

NEWS OF THE OMINOUS INCIDENT REACHES THE BOARD OF DIRECTORS AND CHARLES FRAGE IS IMMEDIATELY SUMMONED!

BUT IF YOU HAD ALLOTTED ME FUNDS BEFORE, THIS NEVER WOULD HAVE HAPPENED!

YOU'RE THROUGH HERE, FRAGE! LEAVE THE UNIVERSITY AT ONCE! YOU'RE MAD!

MAD, AM I?! I'LL LEAVE! BUT YOU'LL PAY DEARLY! YOU FOOLS!

THE ENRAGED FRAGE, SEETHING WITH HATRED, MOVES HIS EQUIPMENT TO AN ABANDONED SHACK CLOSE TO THE UNIVERSITY AND CONTINUES HIS WEIRD EXPERIMENTS!

THEY'LL PAY FOR THEIR FOLLY! THE POWER OF MY FLUID SHALL BE THEIR VERY DOOM! HA-HA!

THE HORRIBLE BAND STRIKES WITH SAVAGE EFFICIENCY AS ITS FIENDISH MASTER WATCHES GLEEFULLY!

BUT THE PROFESSOR'S HOUR OF LURID TRIUMPH IS SHORTLIVED!

THE MANIACAL PROFESSOR RETREATS TO HIS LABORATORY AND IS GREETED BY A SIGHT THAT MAKES HIS BLOOD RUN COLD!

THEY'RE LOOSE! THEY'VE ESCAPED FROM THEIR CAGES!

GRRRRRR

NO! NO! I AM YOUR MASTER! YOUR CREATOR!

AIIEE! NO!

GRRPH!

NO! TRAPPED! THE FIRE! YEEOW!

THE ENTIRE LABORATORY BECOMES A BLAZING INFERNO, THE ROARING FLAMES DEVOUR THE HIDEOUS MONSTERS...!

AGGRRAA!

GRRPPHH!

...AND THEIR INSIDIOUS, FORSAKEN CREATOR WHO DIES WRITHING HELPLESSLY IN THE WEB THAT GRASPS HIM!...THE SPIDER MAN INDEED!

THE WEB! I CAN'T... GET...OUT... (GASP) OF THE...AGGGRRRAAA!!!

THE END.

6

MURDER OF A MONSTER

The sidewalk bubbled and seethed beneath Ted Griffin's feet. It was as though the blistering noonday sun had transformed the concrete pavement into a living volcano, as though a thousand tongues of fire crackled just below the surface, waiting to explode their molten heat right back into the face of the merciless sun. Ted Griffin mopped his streaming face with a dirty, sweat-soaked bandanna, and plodded on.

He tried not to see the emptiness of the streets, tried not to think of the millions of safe, secure people who were luxuriating in air-cooled restaurants and movies and offices while he endured the burning torment of the heat.

He tried to swallow the lump of bitterness that rose up in his throat. Every now and then he glanced at the torn newspaper advertisement clutched in his hand. "MEN WANTED" it said —and the words gave him the strength to go on.

Ted Griffin was just about at the end of his rope. Homeless, jobless, penniless, dirty and hungry! He hadn't had a square meal for almost three days, and his stomach was twisting in protest. Everything depended on his getting this job—*everything!* His very life, in a way...

There was the building at last. He checked the newspaper clipping again, just to make sure. The address was the same. This was it then.

Squaring his shoulders as best he could under his torn and rumpled jacket, Ted Griffin stepped inside. "I—I've come about the job, sir," he told the fat, oily-looking man behind the desk, "the job you advertised in the paper. It said 'MEN WANTED'..."

"Yeah!" The fat man took his cigar out of his mouth and laughed—nastily. "That's what it said all right—MEN wanted—not skinny, scrawny little pipsqueaks like you!"

"But I can do the work, sir!" Ted pleaded desperately, "I know I can—no matter what it is! I'm much stronger than I look! And I need the job..."

"This isn't a charity organization, Skinny!" roared the fat man. "It's a trucking company! And we don't hire tramps! Now, get out!!"

A dull red haze hung before Ted Griffin's eyes. His brain reeled dizzily, unable to focus. Nothing existed but the man behind the desk, the bloated, evil monster who was laughing at his desperation. A monster like that was a menace to the world...he didn't deserve to live...he should be struck down...down...down...

Griffin's hands snaked out—almost as if they had a will of their own. They fastened themselves around the monster's throat—and squeezed. Somewhere a man was screaming... it sounded like the monster's voice...but of course that couldn't be...because the monster's voice was imprisoned in his throat...his thick, fat-creased throat...The hideous snap of his victim's windpipe as it smashed in two jolted Ted Griffin back to reality.

He stared at the jelly-like mound of sagging flesh behind the desk as if he'd never seen it before. "But I'm not a murderer!" he whispered aloud into the stillness—and the walls seemed to catch the echo. "Murderer . . . murderer . . . murderer..." they hissed.

"No! NO!" screamed Ted Griffin, backing towards the door. And then he saw it wasn't the walls at all. A thousand dark and twisted insect-like creatures swarmed towards him. And the rustle of their fangs echoed "murderer."

Blackness descended upon him . . . deep, dark, smothering blackness...a thousand red-hot rapiers pierced his brain...a thousand slimy claws seemed to pluck his soul right out of his body. And over and above it all gurgled the insane laughter of the fat man...until at last the blackness closed about him entirely...like a shroud...

IN A MOMENT OF RECKLESS IMPULSE, MADDENED, FORSAKEN PETER ERLU IMPLORED SATAN TO AID HIM! AND SATAN COMPLIED WITH VIOLENT RAPIDITY AS HE PRESENTED ERLU WITH...

THE Devil's Necklace!

AAGGRRAAA

HA-HA HA HA-HA

NIGHT AFTER NIGHT FROM THE CHEAPEST SEAT IN THE BALLET THEATRE, PETER ERLU LOOKS ON INTENTLY!

SHE IS MAGNIFICENT! IT IS A SHAME THAT GIGI STARLEAU IS ONLY THE NUMBER 3 BALLERINA! SHE SHOULD BE THE FIRST!

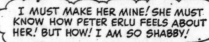

I MUST MAKE HER MINE! SHE MUST KNOW HOW PETER ERLU FEELS ABOUT HER! BUT HOW! I AM SO SHABBY!

EXIT

A NECKLACE FOR ELLEN GAR! AND FROM THE DEVIL HIMSELF! HEE-HEEEEE!

SWOOOOSH!

AGGG-RRRR-AAA....!

HEE-HEE! SPLENDID! ONE LESS OBSTACLE IN GIGI'S PATH TO FAME!

THE NEXT MORNING IN THE LAVISH APARTMENT OF PRIMA BALLERINA ELLEN GAR!

STRANGE! I DIDN'T SEE THIS DELIVERED! WHAT A SUPERB NECKLACE! FROM A BASHFUL ADMIRER, NO DOUBT! I'LL TRY IT ON!

WELL DONE, MY NECKLACE! NOW FOR NORMA RODENNE! HA-HA!

THE BEAUTIFUL DANCER PLACES THE FATEFUL NECKLACE ABOUT HER NECK UNAWARE OF ITS SINISTER ORIGIN OR PURPOSE!

HOW LOVELY! IT'S...IT'S...(GASP) I'M CHOKING...IT'S STRANGLING ME... (GASP)...AIEEE!

NEWS OF ELLEN GAR'S DEATH SHAKES THE ENTIRE BALLET COMPANY TO ITS FOUNDATIONS! AND AS NORMA RODENNE, NUMBER TWO BALLERINA, PREPARES TO ASSUME THE PRIMA DIVA'S ROLE...

GOOD LUCK, NORMA! YOU'RE NUMBER ONE BALLERINA NOW! AND GIGI IS SECOND!

THANK YOU, SIR! I'M GRATEFUL FOR YOUR CONFIDENCE!

3

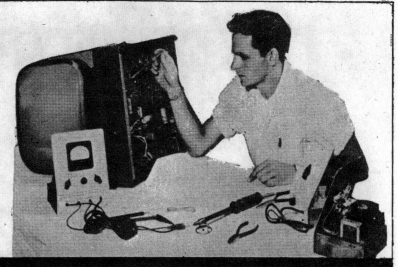

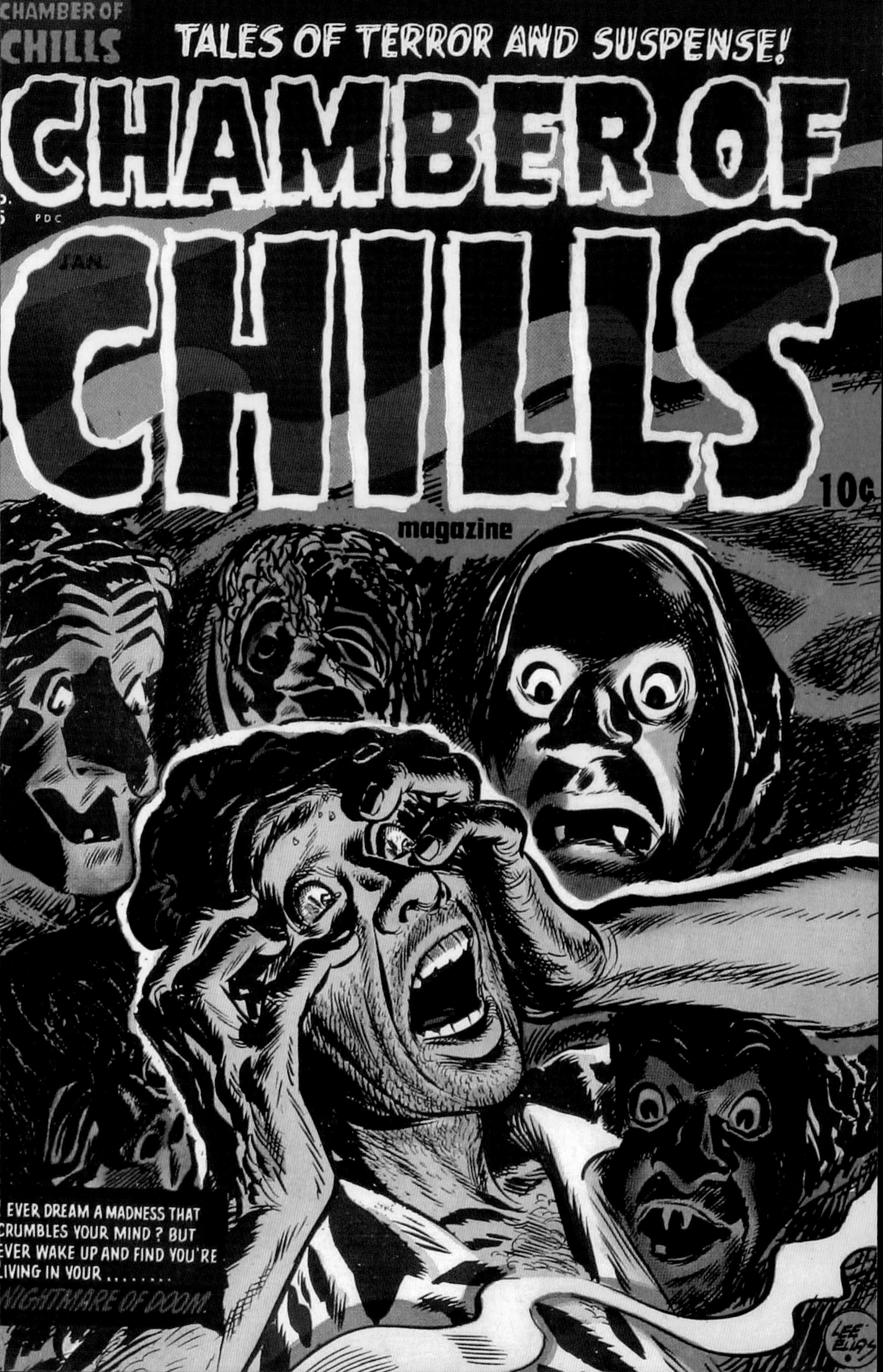
CHAMBER OF CHILLS
TALES OF TERROR AND SUSPENSE!
CHAMBER OF CHILLS
PDC
JAN.
10¢
magazine
EVER DREAM A MADNESS THAT CRUMBLES YOUR MIND ? BUT EVER WAKE UP AND FIND YOU'RE LIVING IN YOUR ....
NIGHTMARE OF DOOM!
LEE ELIAS

WELCOME INTO THE CHAMBER

The flames ... the scarlet, blood-red Devil flames leap high to the sky! Satan shrieks a laugh of evil and throws more fuel to the fire.

Ever-spreading blazes move as chains igniting all in an encompassing sweep. Scalding lava bubbles a bath of horror as the pot overflows its ghastly holdings!

The night is inflamed with the occult ... for you have arrived at the CHAMBER OF CHILLS!

Never before have human eyes seen the terror that lives in these walls! Only now will the dreaded secrets that even demons have tried to forget be revealed!

Amidst the decay and burning evil ... amidst the twisted, weird forms that move in the slime—are stories that tear at the sanity ... scenes that dull the senses!

Satan's call has been answered. All the monsters, spectres, ghouls and zombies that inhabit the land of no return have heard the summoning. Brethren of the forbidden have come together into one loathesome congregation of evil!

Horror has come home ... terror has found its workingplace! The Devil lives in the CHAMBER OF CHILLS!

Now enter Satan's palace. Drink in his special brews. Read the most fantastic stories ever lived. Watch the most grotesque scenes ever imagined. Enter the most amazing magazine ever published! Read ...

CHAMBER OF CHILLS!

WHAT IS IT THAT COMES OUT OF THE NIGHT LIKE SOME APPALLING CREATURE OF HELL AND DEVOURS THE BODY AS IT DERANGES THE MIND?? WHAT IS THIS MONSTROUS CREATION...THIS...

NIGHTMARE OF DOOM!

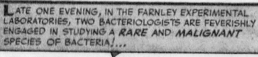

LATE ONE EVENING, IN THE FARNLEY EXPERIMENTAL LABORATORIES, TWO BACTERIOLOGISTS ARE FEVERISHLY ENGAGED IN STUDYING A *RARE* AND *MALIGNANT* SPECIES OF BACTERIA!...

COME SEE THE MOULD, FISK! SEE HOW OUR *LOVELY* CREATURES DANCE UNDER THE MICROSCOPE!

I WISH WE WERE DONE WITH THEM, BARTLETT!

LIKE SOME DEMON WITH A THOUSAND ARMS, THE MASS OF BACTERIA BEGINS TO SPREAD THROUGHOUT THE LABORATORY, *GREEDILY* CONSUMING EVERYTHING IT MEETS--*RAVENOUSLY* RUSHING ON-WARD!...

....AND *ONWARD*...AND *ONWARD*!!...

GOOD LORD!! IT'S AS IF THE BUILDING WERE BEING *EATEN* BY SOMETHING... *LOATHESOME*!!

RUN FOR YOUR LIVES-- IT WILL *NEVER* STOP SPREAD-ING!!

PEER LABORATORIES

OH-H-H-H-H!!

NEAR THE SCENE OF SPREADING HORROR, DOCTOR HUGHES OF A NEARBY BACTERIOLOGICAL LABORATORY WATCHES THE SCENE WITH *SHOCK* AND *TERROR*!...

IT MUST *BE* SOME RARE SPECIES OF BACTERIA THAT CAN GROW AT AN *ABNORMAL* RATE AND THEREFORE SPREAD ITSELF OVER A VAST AREA!!

WE'VE GOT TO DO SOME-THING, DOCTOR HUGHES! THAT DREADFUL MASS CAN *ENVELOP THE CITY* IN A MATTER OF HOURS!!

THERE'S ONLY *ONE WAY*: WE'VE GOT TO CULTIVATE A SPECIES OF BACTERIA OF AN *OPPOSITE TYPE* WHICH CAN DESTROY THE OTHER BEFORE IT SPREADS TOO FAR!

THEN LET'S GET AT IT AT ONCE!

IN A FRANTIC RACE WITH *DEATH*, THE MEN OF SCIENCE LABOR TO PRODUCE THE COUNTER-BACTERIA-- MAN'S *ONE CHANCE* OF SURVIVAL!

DOCTOR HUGHES--YOU MUST HURRY! THE SPREAD-ING BACTERIA IS ALMOST TO *OUR DOOR*!!

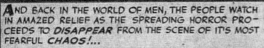

AT THAT MOMENT, THE DEAD MAN'S LAWYER ENTERED THE ROOM...

SO THE VULTURES ARE CROWING --AND HIS POOR BODY NOT YET COLD! I WARN YOU --BUILD HIM HIS TOMB! HE PLANNED ON IT ALL HIS LIFE!

GET OUT OF HERE, YOU DODDERING BOOB!

WE'RE NOT SQUANDERING MONEY ON A TOMB!

TAKE MY WARNING---AND BUILD HIS MAGNIFICENT TOMB! THERE'LL BE PLENTY OF MONEY LEFT FOR YOU! IF YOU DISOBEY HIM, HE SWORE TO RETURN FROM HIS GRAVE FOR VENGEANCE...

HE TRUSTED YOU! SEE? HE SLEEPS IN PEACE! DON'T BREAK THAT TRUST ---KEEP YOUR PROMISE TO HIM!

OUT MEDDLING IDIOT! OUT!

"RETURN FROM HIS GRAVE"--- HA-HA-HA-- THAT'S RICH-- HA-HA-HA!

HA-HA-HA-- WE CAME IN RICH'S-- AND WE'RE LEAVING STILL RICHER!

MONEY-- I LOVE THE STUFF! THERE MUST BE CLOSE TO A MILLION TO DIVVY UP!

WANTING A MAGNIFICENT TOMB-- THE OLD FOOL!

AND SO THE OLD MAN'S TIRED, WORN BODY WAS PLACED IN A SMALL, CHEAP TOMB! DEATH CHEATED HIM OF THE DREAM OF LIFE; HIS GREEDY CHILDREN CHEATED HIM OF HIS LIFE'S DREAM---A LARGE, SUMPTUOUS TOMB...

AH, THEY'LL LIVE TO DIE IN HORROR FOR THIS! HE'LL COME BACK FROM THE GRAVE, AS HE VOWED HE WOULD! HE'LL COME BACK!

THREE CRUEL, GREEDY PEOPLE, THE CHILDREN OF DEAD PETER RICH: OSCAR, A STOCK-BROKER; MAISIE, AN ARTIST, AND STEVE, A TRANSPORTATION EXECUTIVE...

AH, BLAST THESE LATE BOARD MEETINGS! (YAWN) WANT A RIDE HOME, STEVE?

NO! MY CAR IS PARKED JUST ACROSS THE TRAFFIC YARD...

STEVE--*LOOK OUT FOR THAT CAR!*

WHA--? OH-OH! THAT CAR---HAVE TO GET OUT OF ITS WAY...

IT'S COMING AFTER ME--IT'S JUMPED THE RAILS! HELP! *HELLLLPP!!*

HA-HA-HA-HA-HA-HA-HA-HA!

A SLIP OF A FOOT ON THE SLIPPERY TRACKS...A FALL OF A BODY...AND THEN A FINAL SCREAM OF HORROR...

YA-YAAAAAAA--- IT'S HIM!

HA HA HA HA HA HA HA HA HA HA HA

WHAM!

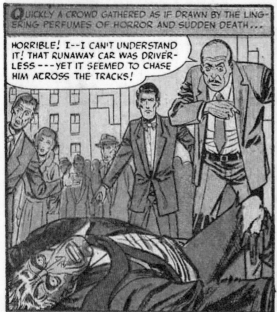

QUICKLY A CROWD GATHERED AS IF DRAWN BY THE LINGERING PERFUMES OF HORROR AND SUDDEN DEATH...

HORRIBLE! I--I CAN'T UNDERSTAND IT! THAT RUNAWAY CAR WAS DRIVERLESS---YET IT SEEMED TO CHASE HIM ACROSS THE TRACKS!

THREE GREEDY PEOPLE...AND NOW THERE ARE BUT TWO: OSCAR, A STOCK-BROKER...MAISIE, AN ARTIST...

THERE! IT'S FINISHED! A LITTLE GRIM---BUT IT'S MY MASTERPIECE!

3

HMM... WONDER WHAT I CAN TITLE THE CANVAS---IT'S NOT EASY TO CHOOSE A FITTING NAME FOR DEATH... NOT EASY AT ALL...

CALL ME ONLY THE VENGEFUL CORPSE, MY DEAR! HA-HA-HA-HA!

YAAAAAAAA!

SURPRISED, EH? COME, COME--- LET AN OLD MAN COME CLOSE TO YOU--CLOSE ---CLOSE! HA, HA, HA, HA, HA, HA!

NO--NO-- KEEP AWAY--- KEEP AWAY!

AND WHERE SHALL I GO? BACK TO MY HANDSOME TOMB? NO! I HAVE COME FOR YOU---COME FOR YOU!

KEEP---AWAAAY--- YAAAAAAAAA...

HA-HA-HA- HA-HA-HA...

THREE GREEDY PEOPLE, AND NOW THERE IS BUT ONE---OSCAR, THE STOCK-BROKER...

POLICE SAY THE ARTIST WAS A SUICIDE! (CLICK!)

STEVE, KILLED BY A STREETCAR--MAISIE, A SUICIDE---ALL IN ONE EVENING! IT ISN'T POSSIBLE! I-- I WONDER IF---IF THAT OLD DEVIL DID RETURN FROM THE GRAVE---

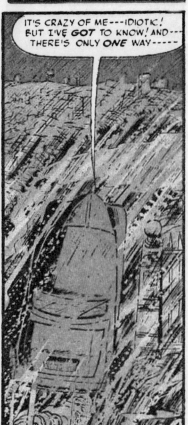

IT'S CRAZY OF ME---IDIOTIC! BUT I'VE GOT TO KNOW! AND--- THERE'S ONLY ONE WAY-----

4

NOW---*NOW*---I'LL LEARN THE TRUTH! IF HIS COFFIN IS EMPTY I'LL KNOW WHO MURDERED THEM! A GHOUL FROM THE GRAVE!

AH-HA-HA--I KNEW I WAS WRONG! *I KNEW IT COULDN'T BE!* YOU'RE DEAD, YOU OLD FOOL---*DEAD!* YOU NEVER CAME BACK FROM THE GRAVE---*NO ONE COMES BACK FROM THE GRAVE!* I'M SAFE! *HA HA HA HA HA!*

WHAT THE---THE TOMB DOOR---THE WIND BLEW IT SHUT---

BOOM!

I'LL JUST YANK IT OPEN AND--OH, NO! *OH, NO! IT'S STUCK! I CAN'T OPEN IT! HELP, HELP---I'M TRAPPED IN HERE!*

THE HOURS MOVED SLOWLY BY AND THE TRAPPED MAN'S FRANTIC SCREAMS AND STRUGGLES GREW WEAKER...FOR THE AIR IN THE SMALL TOMB WAS BECOMING THIN...

GAAAA---AIR---HELP---*GASP!* AIR---GAAA---DYING---NEED AIR---HELP---*GASP!*----

THE HORRIBLE RASPING STRUGGLE FOR BREATH CEASED...AND ANOTHER GREEDY SOUL LAY DEAD IN THE NIGHT...

AND THEN, ON THE COLD, HARD FACE OF THE CORPSE THERE CAME A CHANGE...ONCE AGAIN THE FEATURES BORE A GENTLE SMILE OF PEACE.

5] The End

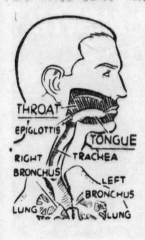

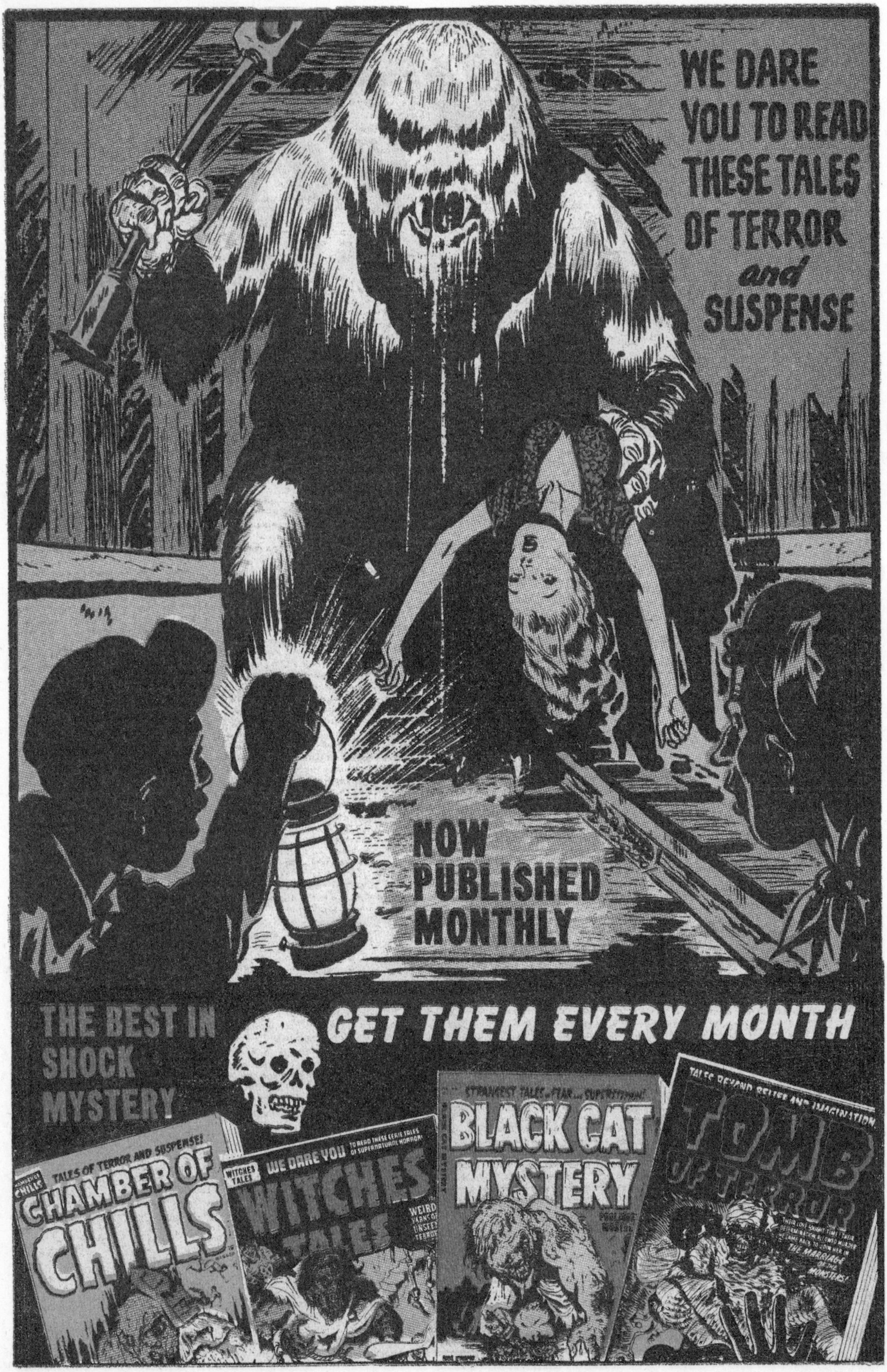

THE PLACE!

"Hurrahhh!!"

Screams of joy pierced the evil chamber as a body was thrown to the flames!

"Aghhhhhhh!"

With each cry for mercy, the horrible creatures danced and sang with glee.

"Aghhh! Aghhhhh!"

A lance was thrown at the inflamed body. And another, and another!

"Stop! Oh, stop!"

Now a ghastly form of a misshapen monster poured a great pot of molten lava upon the rotting man!

"Oh, please end it! End it! Let me die!"

"Let him die! Hah!"

"But you are dead! Hah!"

Throughout the environs similar scenes were going on. The place was a madhouse of mayhem, a charnel house, a torture chamber, an eternity of agony!

"Is it time yet?"

"No, we must wait for Ogar."

"Look! Who is coming in through the cave?"

"It is Ogar! What news do you bring, Ogar?"

"Friends, we can't go through with it! We must not go through with it!"

"Don't talk like a fool! Is everything ready?"

"No! Nothing is ready! I will have no part in this! I have made no arrangements. I have returned here only to tell you that I am through with your plots! I am going to try to leave this place!"

"You're talking madness, Ogar! You know you can never leave this place! You know what awaits you should you dare!"

Hearing this, Ogar picked up a burning torch and threw it at the group.

"I will leave!"

Ogar ran toward the cave, but many of the ghastly creatures followed.

"Get him! Bring him back! Give him no mercy!"

They grabbed him and kicked him. They jumped at him, and tore at him. They seared him with torches, and stretched his body.

Ogar shrieked, screamed, cried in agony . . . but refused to take part in the plans.

"Never! Do what you want to me, but I shall never aid you! You can rot my body, but you have done all you can with my soul!"

"Throw him into the lava pool!"

"Aghhhhh!"

Into the boiling pool went the decaying body of Ogar, and the creatures danced round the site with wild shouts and groans.

"Enough!" said the leader. "Bart, you will take on Ogar's task! Find a friend of ours, and return immediately!"

"I go."

The tumult never stopped while they waited for Bart's return. The gloom and the doom continued to cover the place. Evil continued to boil and boil.

"Make merry, friends! More fuel for the lava! Let the slime run on!"

"Master, I have come back! I am here!"

Ogar dashed through the cave entrance and fell at the feet of the leader.

"Speak, Ogar! Has everything been done?"

"Oh, yes, sire. It was easier than I had expected. All we need is one man to cast his lot with us . . . I have found countless ones!"

"Hah! Hah! I knew that evil did not die! I knew it could never be defeated! The fools who dare to doubt its power will pay for it now!"

"Hurrah!"

"Let us hasten!"

"Cease your shouts," said the leader. "First we must dance the Dance of Doom!"

The bizarre figures of the place whipped themselves into a hideous frenzy. Death was in their eyes! Their feet moved in twisted and weird fashions as the smell of rotting flesh seeped through all.

"Grab the torches! Get the burning spears and knives! Bring the vats of boiling lava!"

"Yes, master!"

"Our day of vengeance has come!"

"Now, make way for me! Open your ranks and let me pass! I must lead the way!"

And the creatures made a path for the leader. His cape fluttered behind him as he proudly walked through, nodding his head to the countless figures as he passed.

"Now we are ready! Burn those flames high! The earth will be ours again! Satan shall recapture his throne!"

FOLLOW US INTO THE HEART OF THE BLAZING DESERT WHERE EVIL LURKS IN THE BROODING SILENCE--WHERE MEN SHRIEK IN PANIC AT THE UNHOLY AND APPALLING SIGHT OF...

THE LIVING MUMMIES

YOU HAVE *DEFILED* THEIR SACRED TOMB--AND YOU LEFT ME TO *DIE* IN THE *DITCH* OF ANTS!! FOR THIS YOU MUST BE *DESTROYED*!!

NO! NO! IT CAN'T BE--*HIM*!! YAAAH-H!!

STUMBLING THROUGH THE *ENDLESS* WASTES OF THE EGYPTIAN DESERT, THREE ARCHEOLOGISTS COME UPON A *STRANGE* AND *STARTLING* DISCOVERY!!

WHY, THIS TOMB MUST BE *THOUSANDS* OF YEARS OLD!!

AND LOOK AT THE ROWS OF *WELL-PRESERVED* MUMMY CASES!!

WE'LL SET UP OUR CAMP NEARBY! I'D LIKE TO STUDY ALL THESE SPECIMINS CAREFULLY!

SO WOULD I, WADE! THINK OF THE DEAD SOULS THAT HAVE BEEN SLEEPING HERE FOR CENTURIES!!

THAT EVENING, IN THE CAMP OF THE MEN, THE SINISTER SILENCE-- AND THE VAST EXPANSE OF NOTHINGNESS--STRIKE SUDDEN FEAR AT THEIR HEARTS UNTIL...

WHERE ON EARTH DID WADE GO?? I TOLD HIM NOT TO WANDER...

AARGHH

A WILD SHRIEK OF AGONY BRINGS FLASK AND HATCHER TO A SIGHT OF UNHOLY HORROR THAT FREEZES THE BLOOD AND MAKES MEN MAD!!

UGH-HHHH! THE ANTS--THEY'RE FEEDING ON HIS BODY!!

FLASK! HATCHER! HELP ME!! AARGH-H-H!!

WH--WHAT SHALL WE DO?? WE CAN'T HELP HIM NOW!

N-NO! THEY MIGHT KILL US TOO! LET HIM DIE!!

WE COULDN'T SAVE HIM, COULD WE? HE--HE MUST HAVE STUMBLED ON THEM IN THE DARK!!

THERE WAS NO POINT IN SACRIFICING OURSELVES!! FORGET ABOUT IT, FLASK!

WE'LL LEAVE HIM HERE--AND BURY HIM IN THE MORNING!

THESE MUMMIES GIVE ME THE SHIVERS! LET'S GET OUT OF HERE!!

LATE THAT EVENING, WITHIN THE SILENT TOMB, A STRANGE STIRRING BEGINS--AND FROM THE DEPTHS OF THE MUMMY CASES, DREADFUL FIGURES EMERGE LIKE SLIMY WORMS FROM A ROTTING CORPSE!!...

OH-H-H-H!!! OH-H-H-H!!!

MY PEOPLE, OUR TOMB HAS BEEN *DEFILED* BY INTRUDERS! THEY HAVE LEFT A *DECAYING CORPSE* ON OUR *SACRIFICIAL ALTAR!* THEY MUST BE *DESTROYED* BEFORE WE CAN RETURN TO THE *BEYOND!!*

BUT FIRST, WE MUST *REMOVE* THE BODY FROM THE ALTAR! IT CANNOT LIE THERE LIKE A *WRETCHED CURSE!*

YES! YES! IT *MUST* BE TAKEN AWAY!!

*S*UDDENLY, A LOW MOAN ISSUES FROM THE *FETID CADAVER* ON THE ALTAR...

AHHH-H-H-H!! *IT IS MOVING!* THE POWER OF THE SACRED ALTAR HAS RESTORED HIM TO *LIFE!!*

HE MUST BE A *GOD!!* LET US *BOW* BEFORE HIM!!

M-M-M-AGH-HH!...

WHAT IS IT YOU WISH, O SACRED BEING?? I AM THE *LEADER* OF THIS TRIBE LONG *DEAD* -- BUT I SHALL OBEY *YOUR* COMMAND!

I SHALL *HELP* YOU DESTROY THE INTRUDERS!! THEY WATCHED THE ANTS DE-VOUR ME -- AND DID *NOTHING!* THEY MUST BE *KILLED!!* TO-NIGHT WE WILL...

*W*ITHIN THE CAMP OF FLASK AND HATCHER, THE MEN ARE UNABLE TO SLEEP...

WHAT A *STRANGE* NIGHT, HATCHER! THE AIR IS *THICK* AND *HEAVY* WITH THE SMELL OF... *DEATH!!*

I'LL FEEL MUCH EASIER WHEN WE'RE OUT OF THIS *LOATHE-SOME* PLACE!

YOU KNOW, I WOULD ALMOST SWEAR THERE WAS--- *SOMETHING...*

LOOKS LIKE A BAND OF *TRAVELLERS!* NOW *WHO* WOULD BE---

3

LED BY THEIR *REPULSIVE "GOD"*, THE SPIRITS OF THE DEAD SUDDENLY APPEAR OUT OF THE DARKNESS -- LIKE *AVENGING DEMONS* BENT ON DESTRUCTION....

IT'S--IT'S *WADE!!* BUT HOW COULD HE BE--AND WHO ARE THE *CREATURES* WITH HIM ???

LET'S GET OUT OF HERE, FLASK!

YOU CAN *NEVER* ESCAPE YOUR *DOOM!* YOU WATCHED *ME* DIE AND NOW THE CURSE OF A *DEFILED TOMB* SHALL BRING *YOU* DEATH!!

WADE! WE DIDN'T *MEAN* TO LET YOU DIE! WE WERE *FRIGHTENED* AND---

NO! NO! LET US GO!!

YAAAH-H-H-H!!!

TAKE THEM!

IN THE *WILD PANIC* OF THEIR FLIGHT FROM THE *GHOULISH* SPIRITS OF THE DEAD, THE MEN STUMBLE BLINDLY ABOUT---RUSHING INEVITABLY TOWARDS A *FEARFUL FATE!*....

DON'T TOUCH ME! LET ME GO!!

YAAIE-E-E-E!!!

SHALL I HELP YOU, HATCHER?? SHALL I TAKE YOU FROM THE *HUNGRY* CREATURES ??? HA! HA! HA! HA!

THE ANTS!! THE ANTS!! AARGH-H-H-H!!

WHAT ARE YOU GOING TO *DO* TO ME ???

I HAVE HAD MY REVENGE! *HE IS YOURS!* DO WHAT YOU WILL WITH HIM!!

4

PLACE HIM WITHIN THIS CASE! IT HAS NOT BEEN *OCCUPIED* FOR MANY CENTURIES!!

YOU *WOULDN'T* BURY ME ALIVE -- IN *THERE*!! YOU *WOULDN'T*!! NO! NO! YAAAH-H-H!

M-M-M-M--AARGH-H-H!!!

YOU CAN OPEN IT--*NOW*!

ONE MOMENT OF *UNBEARABLE TERROR* -- A SHRIEK OF AGONY---AND THEN FLASK'S *SEVERED* BODY HURTLES FORTH FROM THE CASE!...

AN IRON MAIDEN!! AHA! HA! HA! HA! HA!

OUR TOMB IS *DEFILED* NO LONGER!! WE MUST RETURN TO THE *BEYOND*-- TO DWELL IN ETERNITY!!

ALONE WITH THE *CHILLING* ECHOES OF DEAD SOULS, DEVOID OF THE VENGEANCE THAT GAVE PURPOSE TO HIS *CRUMBLING* LIFE, WADE COMES TO A *HORRIFYING* CONCLUSION!....

I--I CAN *NEVER* RETURN TO CIVILIZATION LOOKING AS I DO!! I'M HALF- ALIVE, HALF-DEAD!! THERE'S ONLY *ONE* THING---

IN THE *BROODING SILENCE* OF THE DESERT, A SINGLE *FRIGHTFUL* FIGURE WALKS SLOWLY AND WITH GRIM DETERMINATION TOWARDS THE WELCOME PEACE--OF *DEATH*!....

YOU SEE, MY FRIENDS, I'VE *RETURNED*!! I'VE *RETURNED*!! I'VE *RETURNED*!!

The End

True Tales of the Tomb

During the 1920's, all the world watched with eager and hopeful eyes the Carnarvon explorations in Egypt. The safari crossed the blazing desert sands to open the tomb of Tut-ankh-Amen, one of Egypt's greatest pharoahs!

The expedition had come its long way for scholarly purposes. For days and days they worked violating the warning written on the tomb: Any who violate the sanctity of this tomb shall meet death!

Then in the months that followed, many of those connected with the expedition sickened and died---some in the strangest of ways. Had the pharoah who had lived and died 31 centuries before made good on his curse?

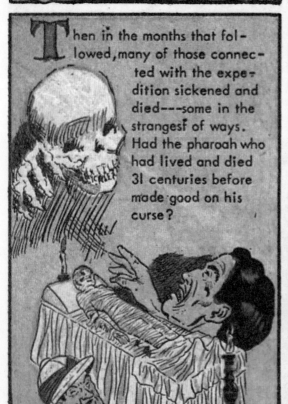

This story does not stand alone. Just a year ago the news agency Reuters reported that four British archeologists died from strange maladies after digging for relics in a forbidden tomb!

BUT SOMEBODY *MUST KNOW* BEFORE I DIE!! IT IS THIS: I HAVE KNOWN THE *METHOD*...THE *RITUAL*...BY WHICH ONE CAN *PROJECT HIMSELF* INTO THE MIND OF ANOTHER TO SEE WHAT *REALLY* LURKS IN THE BRAIN!!

TO KNOW *THAT* SECRET WOULD BE THE *GREATEST DISCOVERY* OF MAN! WHY DIDN'T YOU SPEAK *SOONER?*

BECAUSE THE MINDS --- OF MANY MEN --- ARE TOO *HORRIBLE* --- TOO ---

BUT NO --- I AM SINKING FAST --- YOU MUST *KNOW!* THERE IS A RARE *POWDER* AMONG MY BELONGINGS...ONLY SET IT *AFLAME* IN AN URN AND AS THE SMOKE BILLOWS, REPEAT THESE WORDS: *KORAB DAMORA SHANTU!* THEN -- THEN...

SUDDENLY THE VOICE OF RANJAB AL MARI GROWS *DIMMER*...THE HANDS GROW *COLD*...AND THE FAMED MAGICIAN JOINS HIS ANCESTORS IN THE WORLD BEYOND!...

WHAT IF HIS SECRET IS *TRUE??* IT COULD UNLEASH A *STRANGE NEW FORCE* -- AND YET MEN MUST KNOW ABOUT IT, AND *I* MUST TELL THEM!...

AIEEE!! AIEEEE!!

SEVERAL MONTHS LATER, DOCTOR HARKNESS, GRIMLY DETERMINED TO PRESENT RANJAB'S SECRET BEFORE THE WORLD, APPEARS BEFORE A PANEL OF SCIENTISTS.

...BUT, GENTLEMEN, I HAVE THE *FIRMEST* FAITH IN RANJAB'S REVELATION! YOU MUST GIVE ME THE CHANCE TO PROVE IT!

NONSENSE, DOCTOR HARKNESS, YOU HAVE BEEN DUPED BY A DISREPUTABLE MAGICIAN -- A *LOW FRAUD!!*

ENTER THE HUMAN MIND???

RIDICULOUS!!

ABSURD!!

NO! NO! LISTEN TO ME!! *YOU MUST LISTEN!!*

HA! HA!

I ASK ONLY THIS, DOCTOR PENDLETON: LET ME GIVE A *DEMONSTRATION* OF RANJAB'S THEORY BEFORE AN AUDIENCE OF LEADING SCIENTISTS AND PHYSICIANS!

VERY WELL, HARKNESS, BUT THIS WILL BE YOUR *ONLY* CHANCE!

SEVERAL WEEKS LATER, A *SELECT* BUT *SKEPTICAL* GROUP OF SCIENTISTS GATHER TO WATCH DOCTOR HARKNESS' ATTEMPTED EXCURSION INTO THE *UNCHARTERED REALM* OF THE HUMAN MIND!...

WE SHOULD GO HOME *EARLY* TONIGHT! HE WON'T HAVE MUCH TO SHOW US!

AT LEAST WE MIGHT HAVE A FEW *LAUGHS!!*

DR. PHILIP HARKNESS
VOYAGE INTO THE MIND

...MY FIRST REQUEST, GENTLEMEN, IS FOR A *SUBJECT!* WOULD ANYONE CARE TO VOLUNTEER???

IF THE GENTLEMAN IN THE BLUE SUIT WILL STEP TO THE PLATFORM, I SHOULD BE GLAD TO BEGIN MY DEMONSTRATION!

...IF YOU WISH, DOCTOR!

I AM READY TO START... ARE YOU *COMFORTABLE,* SIR??

YES, YES, PERFECTLY!

SUDDENLY A *GRIM SILENCE* FALLS OVER THE AUDIENCE AND THE MYSTIC SPELL OF THE *UNSEEN* PERVADES THE AIR AS THE STRANGE EXPERIMENT BEGINS!...

I SHALL NOW DROP THIS MATCH INTO THE URN WHICH CONTAINS THE POWDER OF RANJAB AL MARI!

KORAB DAMORA SHANTU!!!

THE SECRET WORDS UTTERED, DOCTOR HARKNESS FEELS HIMSELF HURLED OUT OF TIME AND SPACE INTO A *NEW* AND *FORBIDDEN* WORLD OF THE *HUMAN MIND!*...

YAAAH-H-H-H !!!

WH---I MUST HAVE BEEN *PROJECTED* INTO HIS MIND... AS *RANJAB* SAID I SHOULD BE!! HOW *STRANGE* IT IS! LIKE A *LONG* AND *ENDLESS* PATHWAY!!

SUDDENLY AN *OVERWHELMING* HORROR ALMOST CRUSHES THE DOCTOR'S SANITY AS *APPALLING* AND *LOATHESOME* MONSTERS APPEAR IN THE CROOKED PATH-- SHOCKING EMBODIMENTS OF *EVIL THOUGHTS!!*...

GOOD LORD!!... *WHAT ARE THEY??* WHERE DID THEY *COME* FROM???

SEE! SEE, FRIENDS!! STILL *ANOTHER* VICTIM!!

WE MUST *DESTROY* HIM BEFORE HE ESCAPES!!

LET ME AT HIM!! I SHALL KILL HIM IN A *MOMENT!!* YAAH-H-H-H!!

WITH THE WILD FRENZY OF TERROR, HARKNESS FLEES FROM THE *BLOOD-THIRSTY* DEMONS OF THE MIND... FROM THE *JAGGED* CLAWS AND *ROTTING* HANDS THAT SEEK TO RIP HIS FLESH!...

THIS MAN'S MIND MUST BE... *DEPRAVED!!* HOW WILL I EVER GET FREE OF THIS *MONSTROUS* PLACE?!?

KILL! KILL! KILL!!

4

WEB of DOOM!

"Boris, stop it!"

"Get up, you fool!"

But the creature seemed in another world as he crawled over the carpet, writhing and twisting on the floor!

"Mother, this is the end!"

"Get up, Boris, get up!"

But the misshapen figure continued to creep on his stomach looking down into the patterns of the carpet.

"Hah! Hah! Mother, I'll bet he thinks he's a spider!"

"Boris, you've gone completely mad!"

Still the ugly form didn't hear, but kept on with his ghastly maneuverings.

"We'll have to commit him . . . he'll have to go to the asylum!"

"No! We could never live down the shame!"

Now Boris looked up at the two women and lunged for the mother!

"Go away, you fool!"

She pushed him to the floor, and kicked him in the back again and again!

His face dripped off agony, but he couldn't make a sound. He just retreated to a corner and buried his head in his stomach.

"Push him into the back room . . . with the rats and the lice!"

The daughter obeyed her mother's command and shoved the beastly figure into a back storing room.

"Hah! Hah! So my brother is a spider!"

And slammed the door.

Inside, Boris continued his weird actions. He crawled back and forth across the filthy floor rubbing noses with the spiders!

Once he fell on his back and stayed there for almost fifteen minutes. He fluttered his arms and legs in crazy-like motions until he finally got back on his stomach.

Then he went back to his little friends in the floor's dirt.

Days passed, and the family didn't forget Boris. They kept him locked in the store room away from the light, away from human eyes, but they did feed him.

Each night, Gerta—such was the daughter called—would feed her brother. She'd take scraps from the garbage, rotted flies that had been caught on the fly paper and bones that would otherwise have been garbage. All would be mixed in a pail and shoved inside the room.

Boris would scramble to the mess and devour it all in fifteen minutes.

But one night Boris became restless. He began to crawl hour after hour kicking against the walls, hammering hard on the floor!

"Stop it, you fool!" shouted Gerta. "You will not get food tonight!"

Then Boris became silent.

"All right, my brother. . . Ha, Ha . . . you will get your food!"

She opened the door and threw the pail at the grotesque creature of the floor! The mixture of garbage spilled over all in a blotch of slime.

Suddenly Boris rushed the girl, scratching at her with his nails!

"Keep back, you beast! You spider! Take that! And that!"

She kicked him, and shoved him, and turned him over and over into the slime.

Boris retreated to a corner. But. . .

"Come here, you inhuman beast! I'll kick you till you bleed . . . till you die!"

And she chased him and continued to beat him unmercifully, relentlessly, endlessly . . . till finally he made a sound. . .

"Agghhhhhhhh!!!"

. . . Then he collapsed in a heap on the floor.

"So you can make sounds! Then talk! Speak up!"

She kicked him again . . . but the creature didn't make a sound . . . didn't move.

"He's dead! Ha! Ha! Boris is dead!" The twisted creature was dead. His torment, his loathsome life had been kicked to eternity.

Gerta rushed from the room. Her mother would be glad to know that they were rid of the beast, that they were let loose from the spider's web.

"Mother, come see! I have had the courage to kill him! We are free!"

The two ran to the store room. They opened the door. . .

"Aiiieeeeeee!!!"

Boris was gone. There was nothing but a spider web swimming in a pool of blood!